COLONY THREE

by Christopher E. Cancilla

Cover art by Richard Isbell

https://richard-isbell.myportfolio.com/

In this creative work, any resemblance to any person, from the past, present, or future, living or dead, is pure coincidence.

First Printing

An ever so slight revision

to correct spelling,

grammar, and syntax,

and add a tiny bit of

excitement to the story.

Left blank by design

THANK YOU!

I want to take this opportunity to thank my friends, editors, and a special family. The Battle family you will read about later in this book are friends (not their real names, of course), but it is a tribute to them, a legacy of the love and honor they have….had….for each other. B (in the story) has been a close and dear friend since the 1970s, and her daughter – DROID – is a new friend.

Shay, as always, reads my stories and helps me edit and adjust them in such a way as to make them more exciting and easier to read. I love how she can do that and still enjoy the story. She also said I needed to add certain storylines and elements, and BOY, was she right? I like it better her way.

The history of this story is wild. I started writing this story over a decade ago on a plane, flying home from a contract job in California. I got the idea for the story after looking at the woman sitting next to me on the plane.

A charming and well-featured woman, sound asleep and looking as if she was in suspended animation. Looking at her sleeping, she reminded me of an ancient Egyptian queen. She was barely breathing and completely silent, but something about her prompted me to get this story in my head and start writing it.

As for the Battle family, I wanted to memorialize the B character (you will find out later), as I said, is …. was …. someone I have been friends with since the late 1970s. A coworker in the Air Force and a fellow Munitions Specialist. Her passing affected many people, and this is my way of ensuring she would live on, at least in the story. So when I hear the way the character responds in the story, I can hear her voice in my head saying or doing it or see the look, I mean THAT look, on her face, making me smile.

As I said a moment ago, Shay brought conflict to the story. Initially, I created this story as a perfect place, idyllic. Her logic was that if there was a dark note in the story, it would build interest and offer an alternate plot and a lot of sub-stories. I loved this idea and added multiple points of conflict and negativity in a subtle but noticeable way that adds interest and the ability to take the story, or the sub-story, off on a tangent. Humans are human, after all.

Another piece I added from my initial editors was to have people in the story die over time. Nothing criminal, well, maybe, but the stresses and hardship of space travel are not ignored. The ultimate result, the endgame, of life is death. Not one person can circumvent this outcome; living in other worlds is inevitable after years in space.

I try to show that for each person, position, and job in the story, someone follows behind to learn from the expert and take over when they retire or pass beyond.

I hope you enjoy the story and feel for the characters as I do.

Something else that is kinda interesting. The current Mayor of Youngsville, NC, Fonzie Flowers, cornered me; well, actually, he stopped me at a BBQ cookoff one Saturday and said these words to me.

> "You know. If you wrote all these stories, how hard would it be to put the town (Youngsville) in the story and make it sound like it belongs? Put us on the map!"

I took that as a challenge, and now, Youngsville, NC, is in this book forever. Once I get the book into print, I will take a couple of these books, sign them, and drop them off at the mayor's office.

One last thing. I want to thank Richard Isbell, my brother from another mother, my Air Force friend for the past few decades. Rick is an artist. A damn good one too! I showed him my thoughts on the cover design, and in a few minutes, he created the cover you are looking at in a few minutes!! If you need anything artsy, drawn, graphicly created, or "UPGRADED," please check out his portfolio.

https://richard-isbell.myportfolio.com/

Happy Reading!!

Chris Cancilla

COLONY^3

$$\Delta t' = \frac{\Delta t}{\sqrt{1-\frac{v^2}{c^2}}}$$

Writtten by: Christopher Cancilla

PROLOGUE

Flying through space has become somewhat routine of late. Trips to the lunar surface, Mars, the stations, and the belt make good work trips and a great working vacation. The solar system is much smaller, with Jupiter station open for visitors and the terraforming of a couple of its moons. There is a direct path to the lunar surface using public transportation. The cost is quite affordable, even for a family. From there, you can select a schedule that fits your needs to the stations in the belt, Mars, or the rings of Saturn.

The colonization of the stars is the next human adventure. The closest are the Centauri stars, Alpha and Proxima. However, with a minimal distance of only 4 lightyears, about 38 trillion kilometers, it will take the ships a generation to arrive in orbit of their new home.

Roger Beeker quickly became a household name after the first three colony ships launched a few months ago. Unfortunately, he seems to have vanished after the last ship embarked, and most people suspect he found a way to become a part of the third crew. It was a life he desired, and he created the technology to make it happen.

His design for the stasis tube and the colony ship made it possible for travelers to sleep through the most extended portion of any journey. They saved valuable resources on the flight to and from distant points, like air, water, and food. When they awaken near the destination, it's as though they just woke from a nap.

The ESA, Earth Space Administration, tested the process locally in our solar system. A quick trip to Mars, a few moons of Jupiter, and we cannot forget about Pluto. To the ships' occupants, the trip took maybe 3 days in each direction, regardless of where the crew was destined. The navigation system Roger helped design was flawless on the local scale, in our solar system, and intuitive enough to plot the intercept course for the intended destination, whether it was Mars, Jupiter, the rings of Saturn or the asteroid belt, or our smallest planetoid, Pluto.

On a galactic scale, he estimated a .9% variance. Making it less than a 1% chance of ending up in the wrong place. That means you can end up 26 billion kilometers from your intended destination. In the vastness of space, that is a drop in the ocean, right? To correct this variance, the computer will make a calculation and course correction every few days, which, according to Dr. Beeker, will drop that error rate to less than .001%. This actually calculates out to less than 100 million kilometers. That is two-thirds the distance the Earth is from the Sun. An acceptable margin of error, unless that error drops you in a star.

The most profitable flight was the last flight before the colony ships launched. Maybe 6 years previous, the asteroid belt was the destination. They were looking for gold, titanium, water ice, and frozen oxygen in either O^2 or O^3 flavor. This would become the fuel to return to the Earth from mining the belt and fill the life support systems of those ships, colonies, and stations in space and orbit.

The first trip brought back two metric tons of titanium and gold. Effectively trashing the world economy in one short trip. However, they did find a frozen oxygen ball and refilled their fuel cells before heading home. They found several; actually, one was a few kilometers in diameter. They dropped a beacon on that ice ball, one of the rocks, so they could find it again.

Construction of the Asteroid Hotel is underway. Although not located in the belt for safety reasons, it is close enough so guests can take day trips and stand on the surface of a rock, older than time itself. This hotel is inside a huge asteroid they pulled from the belt and set in place, making it a stationary and safe spot to vacation. The rooms are equipped with screens to simulate looking out a window. The view can be altered to be whatever you want to watch, providing it is local.

The first colony craft to launch, Colony Ship 1, the Nina, launched on April 1st. A few days later, everyone was asleep. As Captain Jonathon Marcos and Chief Medical Officer Helena Wilke of the Nina headed to their sleep chambers for thirty years, the Captain signed off, leaving the last communications to the Chief Medical Officer. The communications of this and subsequent craft are history. School children listen and watch as they depart from Earth space, heading into the big black unknown.

"Orbital Control, this is the final communication from the Captain of the Nina. I will contact you again in about a generation."

“Nina, Orbital Control. Have a good rest. We have you on the scanner and will maintain vigil. Launched April 1st, 2283 – for the record and for all. We expect to hear from you again around the summer of 2313. ”

“Orbital Control, this is the ship of fools, April fools, signing off. We should all be asleep in an hour. Once the doc puts me to bed, she will make her final checks, say goodnight to you, and hit the hay herself.” He cut the transmitter and turned to the CMO, “Well, here we go.”

“Nina, we will be waiting for the CMO to say goodnight. Orbital Control standing by.”

She nodded and escorted him to his chamber, where she put him to sleep. Before she closed his chamber, she kissed him on his forehead. “Mom would have loved this.”

“Us working together?” He replied.

“No, the idea of sleeping for 30 years.” They both laughed. Their mother was gone but not forgotten.

“She did like her naps!” The Captain, the older brother by 18 months, smiled at his little sister. “Who would have thought the little girl and her dorky brother would be commanding the first long-term mission to another star system to set up a colony.”

Together, they both said, “MOM!” They smiled at each other. She closed the tube and activated the process, watching him begin his long slumber. She took a small piece of paper from her pouch and scribbled a note. She taped it on the glass above his face with the words facing inward so he would see it when he opened his eyes in a few decades.

When planning for this mission, it was decided early on the participants needed to work together for a long time, like forever. So, if possible, family members with needed professions will be looked at first over those who are not related in some way to others on the team. That does not disqualify the single person but puts them on a secondary list. For all three crews, it worked out that every person who applied and some who were asked made it on the team. No one who wanted to go was left behind.

Helena headed to her stasis chamber, which was located next to her husband's tube. She kissed him passionately before activating his chamber, "That needs to last you 30 years."

"That's a long time. If everyone is asleep, maybe we…." He said, grinning.

"You are such a dirty old man." She smiled and kissed him again. "Damn…." She said, "I may take you up on your offer." She hit the activate code, and he settled back, closing his eyes. He smiled and attained oblivion as she watched, ensuring all systems were nominal. One more glance at her husband of more than a decade. He had that grin mounted permanently on his face. The one that makes her melt.

She shook it off and turned around. Before activating her chamber, she sat at her desk, her console. Then, flipping a toggle, "Orbital control, I am the only one awake, and in 10 minutes, I will also be asleep. So, I will hit the hay after one final pass of the ship's systems, stasis tubes, and medical scanners."

"Doctor Wilke, Orbital Control. As the current commander of the mission, since you are the only one still awake, do you have any words for the history books?"

She thought about it briefly and replied through the comm system, "I do. Humanity is branching out. Time to spread our wings. We leave our family and friends behind…no, not behind; we travel far from our family, friends, and fellow humans to start a new humanity. Take care of our home. I plan to return one day and want to see that big blue marble I am looking at. I want to thank Mother Earth for giving me the most beautiful and peaceful view of Earth, one I can implant in my memory and dream about for three decades." She captured the view on her screen and sent it to Orbital Control to let them see what she saw. She paused momentarily to let the sound bite end, "Orbital Control, this is Doctor Helena Wilke. All systems are in the green. I'm beginning to feel a little tired. Perhaps I'll lay down and take a nap."

A new voice appeared, "Helena, you earned that nap. So take it, enjoy it."

She smiled and turned to the display screen to see her old and dear friend and mentor, "Doctor Michaels, I feel privileged. You came off the golf course just to say goodbye to me." She laughed a little, as did he.

"Yes, I did. But you need to know I would not do that for anyone on the little planet."

"Thank you. But in case you are unaware, I am not currently on the planet."

"OK, got me there. Be safe, my friend." He replied back to her, blowing her a kiss, and she returned it. They both laughed softly since the communication was two-way, like a standard vidphone. It was a genuine conversation.

She took a breath, "Orbital Control, this is the Chief Medical Officer of the colony ship, Nina. We are on computer nav heading to Proxima Centauri. All ships' systems are well in the green. We have 287 sleeping souls aboard, young and old, tall and short, with various nationalities, colors, and professions. The perfect sampling of Earth. In a few minutes, it will be 288 in stasis."

"Good night, Helena. Rest well. We will talk to you again in a few decades." There was a dramatic pause, "Nina, this is the president of your homeworld, Michael Ross. I want to bid you a safe flight and a good rest, and let you know all humanity is holding their collective breath."

"Thank you, Mr. President."

"Nina, Orbital Control. Have a good sleep. Orbital Control out and standing by."

"Orbital Control, Nina. The sleep program is running. The ship is on full computer control. Dr. Beeker, I pray that your nav calculations are at least close. Of all the things that can go wrong, ending up in the wrong place for some reason is my greatest fear. Thank you for everything. Nina out."

The Chief Medical Officer and her husband were the last to enter the long sleep. He is her #2 in the medical department.

He was already sleeping. The two ran the medical team on the ship and will resume that duty when they get to the planet.

Helena is a general practitioner specializing in family medicine and treatment. As she likes to put it, cradle to grave. She may not be an expert, but she is trained in multiple specialties.

In contrast, her husband, Ralph, is the most sought-after surgeon in North America. The two practiced in northeast Ohio – part of the Cleveland Clinic system.

Along with the two Wilke family members, a few more doctors, nurses, physician assistants, and nurse practitioners round out the medical department. 75% of the colonists had advanced medical training, with the other 25% trained as basic EMTs. Safety first!

Helena put all ship systems on standby, initiated the slumber program in the main computer, and sat in her chamber. This stopped the airflow but maintained an ambient pressure of 40k pascals, roughly half that of Earth at sea level. It also holds a 15% oxygenation. Once the ship reaches its destination, it ramps up the pressure and oxygen for thirty minutes, then wakes the primaries of the crew to verify they are where they should be. Looking around, she smiled, "I'm really doing this?"

Lying flat on her back, she pressed the blue button, closing the chamber. She felt the transition into stasis; it was odd momentarily as she closed her eyes. She was asleep.

~~~~~~~~~~~
~~~~~~~~~~~

As the ship successfully entered the system as envisioned, the ship's computer woke the set of doctors, who revived the primaries of the crew as scheduled.

Helena opened her eyes and wondered if this was it or if she had just laid down. A quick glance at the chronometer in front of her tells her she has been asleep for 31 years, 243 days, 23 hours, and a few seconds. She glanced at the status light, green. This means pressure and oxygen levels outside the tube are nominal. She went to move and realized her muscles hurt. She said out loud, "Freezer burn?" and laughed a little. She lay there for a few minutes doing some isometric exercises she told everyone to do before they tried to get out of the tubes. Enough to realize it really hurt and sufficient to get the muscles operational again.

As the Captain woke, he saw the note and laughed. 'Don't be late for school!' the message said. Exiting the chamber, he picked up the scrap of paper and carefully put it into a pocket. That note was 30 years old, he thought.

Once Helena verified no one had any side effects from stasis, the 3 staff members determined the vessel had arrived at the correct location.

"Well, sis, it looks like we will all be on time for school today," Jon said to his sister.

"We're here?" She smiled.

"We are. Thirty-one years, eight months, and three days to be exact. That puts us at September 1, 2314. Around breakfast time since I am hungry after my nap. Wake the medical team in a few hours." He smiled at her, "First, you must shower. Trust me on that!" She nearly started laughing, “After you feel human again, grab some food, and then wake your staff.” It was their role to ensure no problems during crew revival. She was having difficulty walking, but with each step, it is improving. “Oh, I hear from the lady doc that you must drink lots of water when you first wake up.”

“Good idea. I think I will, but I really need coffee. Feels like it’s been decades since my last cup!” She said to him.

The navigators in the room all groaned at the joke.

“What’s water?” She said to him as she left the room.

After she was refreshed, she logged into her system and started the medical stasis chambers to cycle awake. She gave them her brother's orders: shower, eat, and then we would wake everyone else up.

Leaving one chamber to manually open, she approached and pressed the magic button. The chamber changed color slightly, and she saw REM and a slight inhale. She popped the lid as he was recovering. He opened his eyes and looked at her with intense love. Then, clearing his throat, he asked his wife, “Are we there yet?”

His first words in a new solar system. Memorable! She laughed out loud.

They revived the remaining colonists, just under three hundred, and prepared to land the ship a few days later. Everyone needed to regain their legs before they had natural gravity to contend with again. They were to create a human society and infrastructure on the surface of a world they set out for three decades earlier. Hopefully, they will make life in a distant world endurable and survive.

Knowing it would take about four years for a radio signal to reach home, the captain opened the connection and transmitted a message. "Set the transmitter to maximum power and set the directional antenna to intercept Earth."

"Set," came from behind him.

Pressing the key, "Orbital Control, Sol System, Earth." He paused and cleared his throat, speaking louder, "Earth, this is the Nina. We arrived on station Alpha Centauri. Thirty-one years, eight months, and three days after departure. According to your calendar, if my calculations are correct, today is September 1, 2314. We have experienced no issues; all crew members are well and awake. All animals are asleep and in the green. However, during transit, a micrometeorite had a minor impact that transected the ship and somehow managed to miss anything critical. The ship's hull sealed itself perfectly, and the damage was repaired. The meteorological data is currently being reviewed. All 26 probes are still active, as is Genesis. I know you will not receive this message for a few years, four actually, but I wanted to send it regardless. This message will repeat once every 5 minutes for the next 72 hours. After that, we will attain planetfall. The data ARC will be active as soon as possible after landing, so you will hear from us years before you receive this message."

Each member of this mission understood that survival was not guaranteed. The hardest of all possible decisions was not hurling yourself through space in the hopes you would survive to get to the destination three decades later. But make that decision for your children accompanying you on this journey.

The crew consisted of children aged one to the oldest at 57. But, first, they would need to establish a school, and the colony leader had that set well before launch.

18 months from the arrival of Ship 1, the bulk of the colony is scheduled to arrive. The Pinta was expected to depart Earth 18 months after Ship 1, and this ship was quite a bit larger and better stocked for long-term survival. The Pinta, including the additional livestock, doubled the number of humans and contained an extensive supply of seeds.

In addition, it held the bulk of the medical department, including the diagnostic and surgical equipment Nina was not carrying. The Pinta also had three times more medical staff than the Nina, rounding out the medical team. Each ship carried a complete veterinary practice because animals would be necessary in this new world. In addition to several veterinary doctors and a flock of nurses/techs, which ensured everyone could have bacon and eggs for breakfast, the farm-type livestock was more critical for survival. Pets are more important for emotional survival. Dogs, cats, and rabbits are essential, but in reality, a chicken contributes to a bacon and egg breakfast, but a pig gives his all.

Once Ship 2 arrived, they reached the planet and contacted the colony. Touching down a few kilometers away with the hope of starting a second city.

The Pinta launched on schedule and arrived in orbit of the new home planet of this colony as scheduled, more or less. However, they have taken a few additional months to reach their destination. They launched just under 19 months after Nina and arrived 10 months after their expected arrival. Not bad! Their beacon has been on track and watched since the ARC was active. The satellite was placed into orbit to monitor surrounding space, the stars, the radiation levels, the weather on the planet, and a few other things. Genesis still maintains a watch on the people of Earth, transplanted to a distant world. So far, the planning teams have accomplished their goal. One ship remains to arrive.

Colony Ship 3, the Santa Maria, was scheduled to depart 11 months after the Pinta. The third and last ship in this set contained the same number of colonists as the previous 2 ships combined and an impressive array of animals, including dogs and cats from various breeds. Not a single species was turned down. Temperament, mood, loyalty, and attentiveness were the key to the pets. The other ships also carried pets, mostly family pets. This ship collected dogs and cats from shelters on the East Coast of the United States and gave them a home on another planet. All animals were kept in stasis until after landing and not awakened until it was their time.

The ships all carried a complete manufacturing section, including heavy equipment, various generators, and the ability to create refined metals into whatever was needed once on the planet.

The members of the Nina and Pinta discovered Ship 3, the Santa Maria, launched 14 months after Ship 2, a few months later than planned due to the logistics of getting all that livestock and cargo from the surface to the orbital shipyard. It appears that the rescue pets were the longest delayed. Designing their stasis chambers and creating one for each took longer than planned. So, for the past year, the colony – ships 1 and 2 – has been hoping to hear from them. Ship 3 was long overdue to arrive.

The Santa Maria was destroyed or severely off course somewhere out in space. Their beacon was not on any scanner. So they were considered lost to the great empty. All that anyone prayed for was they either died quickly or landed on a planet where they could survive.

Each ship could create a society upon landing, with Ship 2 having an easier time than Ship 1 and Ship 3 being the easiest. In addition, each ship carried a larger quantity of 'something' to distribute to the colony when they arrived.

Colony 1 contained the infrastructure basics, including solar-powered construction and transport vehicles, communications equipment, and security technology. Their primary mission was to land, develop the layout of the new colony, and begin setting up the homes and factories needed to ensure the remainder of the colonists would have a place to live and work. They had 18 months to prepare for Colony Ship 2. The Pinta carried more home supplies than the Nina, who brought more industrial supplies and equipment.

They did have a sufficient quantity of livestock and seeds to feed their minimal population. Still, they were waiting for the other ships to arrive to enhance what they had or did not have. Their first priority was to construct the communications array and contact Earth. It took them longer than expected, a few months, due to the terrain and the fact they needed to find the raw materials to make what they needed.

Many centuries ago, this planet was struck by a large rock. A rock mainly made of iron and gold. They had found the raw materials they needed to create their society.

There were a lot of relieved sighs when that first call from Colony One came through a few months after landing. The data ARC was established a couple of weeks later, making all voice and digital communications available. A week after that, visual communications were turned on. They got used to the 11-second lag in voice/visual transmissions. Still, it worked for the distance between the transmitter and receiver.

Colony 2 arrived 28 months later and carried prefab building materials, the bulk of the seeds, and the livestock. Enabling the colony to survive and thrive. With the arrival of the second ship, the settlement added 301 humans to the 288 already there. That number is increasing faster than anticipated since people are pairing up.

Once the data ARC was established, the first crew learned the Yellowstone Park volcano erupted in a massive explosion less than a year after Ship 3 launched. Earth was in a nuclear winter as they slept. New technology was developed, and space technologies were essentially shelved. It was a hard reality pill to swallow; their home was in ruins, but they accepted it and moved on. Once the Pinta arrived, they relived the discovery of Yellowstone all over again with the new colonists.

Earth developed the orbital Elevator, and in the 30 years the colonists slept, it was built and became the best way to get into orbit. It provides continual power from the massive solar array in Earth's orbit. The Lunar Colony beams energy back from the Moon. The array in Earth's orbit is in constant sunlight, as is the variety on Earth's Moon.

The Orbital Elevators, the Brazil and the Africa Lift are located in Brazil and Kenya. In establishing the lift near the equator, the centrifugal force ensures continuous stability in the facility and the orbital platform.

The Oriximiná Brazil lift is located in the Parque do Tumucumaque in the State of Pará. The facility is near the center of the triangle and is formed by three cities: Tiriós, Trios, and Akotipa. It is located in a somewhat mountainous area, in a basin formed by the mountains. The basin is nearly 2 kilometers across and built into the solid rock bed of the nearby mountains. This facility took longer to create since the roads and infrastructure needed to be completed first. A power plant was built nearby to offer continuous power to the facility. This facility is nicknamed the OB Lift.

The Kalambani Kenya Lift is located in the northeast corner of the South Kitiu National Reserve, roughly 200 kilometers from Mount Kilimanjaro and 200 kilometers from Nairobi. This was the first lift created and, as such, was the primary cargo and personnel lift to the orbital platform. It has since converted to 100% people. It is the primary lift for anyone heading to orbit or transferring to the Lunar or Mars colony. The facility is nicknamed the KK or K2 Lift.

As the colonists came out of stasis, the colony called themselves Terra as an homage to their homeworld; they received data and information on their new home.

The location where the first ship touched down was partially determined before departure and partially determined after arrival in the system. As the colony leadership scanned and reviewed the orbital probe data for the past 30 years, they realized two of the 4 locations designated as landing zones were downright nasty. Torrential rain and severe storms occur most of the year. One was a bit arid, negating the possibility of a bountiful harvest. The fourth was like living in central Canada, with wilderness and lower temperatures.

After reviewing the data, they found that a fifth location was the best. The temperature averaged 23°C with swings from -2°C to 39°C. Rainfall was a moderate 120cm over 2/3 of the planetary year, giving the colony the nickname Seattle. They did receive snow for a month, but the snowfall averaged 50cm, so nothing too terrible or dangerous. Plenty of trees were available for firewood, building materials, the occasional bonfire, and shade from the summer's heat.

Terra was tilted on its axis less than Earth by about 6 degrees, providing their chosen temperate zone. It was, however, farther from a much larger star. As a result, they felt a lot better after testing the probe's data for radiation.

The probe set was launched a few decades before the first ship departed, as they were being built. The vessel received the data and processed it only a few months before arriving in the system. Once they woke up from their slumber, the ship assimilated decades of data and was prepared to present its findings to the crew.

The Genesis 1 probe had 26 additional miniature probes designated Genesis A through Z, which launched into the atmosphere a few days after arrival at the planet. Probes 1 through 9 deployed around the planet and maintained watch over solar radiation and a proximity scan for surrounding space.

Genesis 1 remained in geostationary orbit over the north pole, and the orbital probes connected to all 26 probes on the surface. This point was chosen to allow it to receive solar radiation data and watch for the Colony Ships as they approached; it also gave Earth a clear shot at transmitting data bursts.

The letter probes provided environmental surface conditions around the planet and at the poles upon landing. In contrast, the orbital probes maintained surveillance of orbit, surrounding space, and a reasonable distance into the solar system. When Colony Ship 2 approached, the probes notified the colony a short time before the communication from the ship itself.

Data such as rain, temperature, pressure, and humidity gave the planet a meteorological history. Still, it tested for oxygen, carbon dioxide, monoxide, and sulfur levels. In addition, the probes tested for various toxins, radiation, and allergens common on Earth, but who knows what they will find here? So Genesis was significant, and the designers had a sense of humor.

Genesis 1 looked like an old late 1960s Volkswagon van. They even painted it with peace signs and flowers. The letter probes were the diameter of a serving platter and half a meter tall. It had eight legs and traveled like a giant yellow and blue spider. Each spider had a name on its back, beginning with the letter of its designation. The perfect location for the colony was at the site of probe OWL. The colonists put the probe on a pedestal in the center of the settlement and built a park around it, naming it Owl Square at Town Center.

These readings enabled the colonists to make an educated choice for the location of the new colony; the probes would operate for as long as the power cells lasted, and the solar batteries would recharge the systems as long as the probe was in sunlight. It was estimated that the probes would survive several decades, 4 or 5, and much longer with the colonists' maintenance.

Marcus Samuel, the colony leader, and his family were builders before they departed the solar system. They had an engineering and construction company that Beeker contracted to build the Nina, the Pinta, and the Santa Maria. They made the ships to spec but added a great deal of disassembly capability, knowing that those ships would become their homes and structures when they arrived. When they went into stasis, their company reverted to a group led by the one person in the universe they could trust.

Jackie Bovee, Marcus' sister-in-law, and her husband had business savvy. They did not understand construction but understood, all too well, how to manage the business. They turned over all operational control to them and hoped it was still a business when they first contacted home. They were not disappointed.

Marcus and his wife, Kathryn, had their education in the physical and mechanical engineering areas. Doctorates in both, but they enjoyed one more than the other. Marcus is in Mechanical Engineering, and Katheryn is in Civil

Engineering. She is the primary colony designer and could not begin until they arrived.

They had tenure at their alma mater, the University of Alabama at Tuscaloosa, as they were seasoned professors at the school. They hoped to head the engineering school on their new homeworld one day. In addition, they brought their three children with them from Earth. Martha, age 20, and Victor, age 17, had careers after arrival. 17 was determined to be the best age to be considered an adult, where work and internship were a part of the norm. In contrast, Marcus, Jr., age 14, already had his career in mind. He planned to take over for his father one day.

The ship captain was destined to be the leader of the security detachment and the police force, and Marcus was slated to lead the colony once they landed. It was done this way so the prevailing attitudes would not be military but civilian. Each of the ships had a predetermined military and civilian leadership element. All crew members were aware and had a vote before launch on who would be the civilian leadership and their colony's direction in the future.

Martha had just completed medical school and her internship before launch. She was, is, a doctor, albeit freshly minted at 20, soon to be 21. Nevertheless, she was assigned to medical and would finish her on-the-job education under Dr. Radika Metalia, the Colony Two Medical Officer. Dr. Metalia, having a great deal of teaching experience, was selected by Dr. Wilke as the lead educator for the colony. She has begun a training program more by experience than by books. However, books are necessary to learn the basics. Those interested in joining the medical field apply. Once accepted, you begin the journey; EMT, nurse, and a few doctors. Martha Samuel completed her training more for confidence than education in just a few months. She is a valuable member of the medical school staff and the lead trainer under Dr. Metalia. Now a 24-year-old doctor, plus 31 years in stasis, she loves her job and calling and enjoys passing that knowledge on to those willing to learn from her.

Victor, their middle child, had little interest in specialized education and opted to be 'manual labor,' as he called himself. As a result of that decision, he was classified as non-skilled labor, the backbone of any society, and a jack of all trades, the colony handyman.

If an area is short-handed or needs additional assistance, they call on him, teach him what he needs to accomplish the task, and let him loose on the assignment. He learns fast and learns well. He has worked in every area of the colony and amassed a great deal of knowledge of all forms of maintenance.

As a result, he is familiar with all professions and is friends with all inhabitants. Frequently, Marcus consults with him to find out if there is anything one department has that another department needs. It has proven to be a fantastic opportunity. As such, Marcus created the Colony Maintenance Logistics Department, CMLs, or CAMALs. The positions are filled with Victor and a few others. Their nickname is the HANDYS, and they love that name for themselves. They are following him on his career journey. They learn something new almost every day and have fun doing it. These people like change, making a difference, and the daily feeling of accomplishment, from digging ditches to installing antennas, painting a room, and babysitting. This department does whatever is needed cheerfully. Victor and his team, a team of 14 now, meet weekly to discuss what they learned during the past week. They also decided to take on a name for their department, the Servants. They serve the colony cheerfully, smiling, in whatever capacity they are asked.

They are gaining a following, and Victor's fiance, Gloria, has taken on the coordination task. Although Victor is not interested in management, he wants to do the work, so he is happy she took on that role. Gloria has an office near the Governor's, and when someone is needed, they call her, and she assigns a Servant. She has seen fit to create a training jacket for each of the Handys, and as they learn something new, they let her know, and she adds it to their training jacket. She can input the skills for a task, and qualified names pop up on her screen.

On the other hand, Marcus jr wants his father's job one day, and throughout the 14 years of his life, he has learned and experienced as much leadership as he could. So, one day, he would definitely be the colony's leader. He is smart. Maybe too smart. At 14, he completed high school with an associate's degree in management before leaving Earth. He is nearly 17 now and looking forward to having his own career.

At first, those he worked with did not take him seriously because of his age. Now, he is a valued member of the colony. Although he could take on a managerial position, he chose to be an assistant and learn from the experience of those he worked with. As a result, everyone likes him and helps him understand the what and why of the job, not just the how.

The second in command of the colony, Tonya Waynor, and her husband, William, are technologists. Tonya, the planetwide expert in programming languages, and Willie, the planetary expert in electronics. Between the two of them, they lead technologists and create the needed tech to accommodate their needs. As the scientific leaders of the community, they were responsible for setting up all communications and ultimately positioning the reactor so it could be used as a power source for the entire area surrounding the community.

The power distribution array needed to be high enough to be accessible by all but not so high in the air to detract from the landscape's natural beauty. As a result, the setup is perfect and somewhat concealed. It does not mar the beauty of the relatively spartan planetary landscape.

Tonya and Willie have no children, nor will they ever. They did, however, bring their fur babies with them. 3 dogs, 3 cats, and a family of hamsters. The sign on the door to their home says, 'Welcome to the Zoo.'

The veterinarian on the planet has also taken on a huge responsibility. Knowing she is the colony head vet, with her good friend and former classmate Michael Ramon, they share all duties and work. There is no competition between any profession on this planet. Everyone works well together. As far as anyone is concerned, it is a utopia.

Michael was the lead vet for the Pinta, and Marsha Cassellari was the lead vet for the Nina. Unfortunately, Marsha's twin sister was the lead vet for Santa Maria, and the loss of the third colony ship has not affected Marsha in the least. She seems to feel her sister is doing well somewhere. Somewhere out there. The three graduated from vet school and worked together for a few months before applying for and receiving an appointment to the Colony Ships.

Marsha has focused on pets, while Michael focuses on livestock. They share the office and the facility and can focus on their passion while at the same time backing each other up. They also share a home, and Marsha asks him if marriage is in the stars. He smiles and hands her a ring he made from some of the gold they found. They have been married for 6 months.

With 65 dogs, 90 cats, 34 hamsters, assorted rabbits, ferrets, and other Earth-based pets on the surface, and the number is increasing rapidly, Marsha has a full-time job. Michael has a flock of every ranch animal imaginable, carried on ship 1 and ship 2 and dropped on Terra for the benefit of all. His work day can be long, and he loves his job and wife, who will assist him when needed.

Providing everyday food for your pet or pets was the only requirement when applying to bring your pet on this journey. Your pet or pets came with you, and the food you packed needed a 6-month supply and was stored in the hold. Once on the surface, the pet would start with a total of their regular food and slowly move to 100% of the locally made pet food. There were three types of pets, at least foodwise.

Carnivore, herbivore, and omnivore. The mix was tested on Earth and developed quickly in the colony environment. Mixing in local plants and animal proteins to supplement the lack of specific vitamins and minerals, the animals got used to it and thrived.

On the three-decade-long journey, the animals had their own sleep tube. The vet ensured they went to sleep properly. Since the smallest stasis tubes were still pretty large, smaller critters shared. Cats with cats, hamsters with hamsters, and so on. One family, the Waynors, put all their pets into one stasis chamber. They all knew each other and decided if they lost one, it would tear them apart, but no more so than if they lost them all, all or nothing. They nearly cried when they started to wake up and grabbed their hoomans!

Pets were brought out of stasis after landing and after the family homes were set up. This would create the least stress for the pet in the new environment. Farm animals and the guard dogs were brought out of stasis once their abodes and pens were built. Since they received a mild sedative before stasis, roughly sleeping for six hours on the injection. They woke between 4 and 5 hours after being removed from the tube. This made transfer safer for all concerned.

The Nina and the Pinta colonies are thriving, succeeding, and happy.

CHAPTER ONE

People leave you alone on the night shift, and you get to do as you please when there is no urgent or scheduled work. However, being the #2 Communications Tech on the planet does have perks. The span of humanity on this world encompassed maybe 50 kilometers, so….

Romeo Rodriguez volunteered for the night shift and liked the alone time in the control room. His rating was Communication Technician level 9, the second-highest on this planet. His position was assistant communication manager.

He had full access to everything, but they needed a way to differentiate between him and Wilomena Dumont, his boss, who held level 10. It was as good as solved if the two worked on a problem together. The 9 vs. 10 really meant nothing. It was strictly for accounting created by the governor when they arrived. Since no one was paid currency or salary, it meant more meetings. At least, that is what Romeo tells his boss all the time.

Wilomena was the lead on the Nina, colony ship #1, and Romeo was the lead on the Pinta, colony ship #2. She set it all up and got it all working before he thawed. Romeo was happy to let her take the lead title. It meant fewer meetings for him. He really likes doing the work and not managing.

Supervisors are all level 10, directors are level 20, vice managers are 30, managers are 40, and governors are 50. If desired, the numbers in between can be used to establish a ranking system. A few departments have done this, but more have not. As a result, everyone in a work center knows who the person 'in the know' is and who is still learning.

Marcus created the position of mayor and assigned level 49, letting everyone know precisely where they stood in his eyes. So naturally, placing Tonya in level 49 meant a lot to her and everyone else.

Locally, the planetary year was close to Earth's, short by a few days, according to the astrophysicists. The day was close to Earth's, 22 hours more or less. So rather than trying to break shifts into three like back home, they opted for two shifts of 11 hours. He and Wilomena decided to lead the opposite shifts, mainly because the best person was already involved in the solution if something happened. Because of the little more than 22-hour days, they needed to add a few hours every few years. That is coming up soon for their first timeslip, as they call it. If they did not do this, eventually when, the sunset would be mid-morning.

The advantage of the dark shift over the light shift was that if you wanted to call home to Earth or sit and watch the news, you could, and no one would care. Unless they reviewed the logs, of course. However, the colony leaders never prevented colonists from communicating with the home. Where they landed on the planet had a similar day and night to that of the United States East Coast. So, when calling home, they knew what time it was there. That, along with the display in your residence, has the current time for whatever time zone you want to display.

Tonight, Romeo reviewed the video feed from around the tool shed, where most of the tools were stored in the colony. Unfortunately, things in the past week have gone missing, and no one will own up to borrowing them. "Is someone stealing?" He said to himself. "That is just plain weird. If you need something, sign it out and use it. Why in hell would someone resort to stealing."

For nearly an hour, he reviewed and watched movies. Then, as he was examining the video, he noticed a silhouette walk in and out of the building at a time when it was supposed to be secured.

He tried to improve the video quality and zoom in, but nothing came out. Romeo jotted down a note to review the surrounding cameras as soon as the news was completed because tonight, Romeo decided to watch the news feed as it was received. I guess you could call it live.

It is beamed from Earth during his shift and rebroadcast multiple times when most colonists are awake. The advantage was he watched the program as it was downloaded from the ARC. Recently, he has been very interested in watching commercials that air during programs. Being in stasis for 30 years is hard. Most people you knew had died or forgotten about you, but it seemed like yesterday for you. But, of course, that and technology drastically changed in the last three decades. It all seemed like some futuristic novel or movie plot to him.

Once Yellowstone blew up, the silt covering the entire planet made it close to dark at noon. The dirt and silt encapsulated the northern hemisphere for several days before going below the equator. It made the entire planet unsuitable for growing food and unsuitable for livestock. So space tech changed to survival tech, warehouses, hydroponics, and giant buildings with many lights to simulate day for the animals.

Romeo discovered he had lost a few friends. They were camping in Yellowstone at the time of the eruption. It took him a while to dig into those messages, but all his mail awaited him once the ARC connected. Everyone received massive amounts of messages and correspondence over the three decades they slept. It was stored in the ARC.

Flipping the monitor switch, he had the live stream on the main viewer, an entire wall in his office. He could control anything from here, with his access in the office shared with his boss. Both of their desks faced the screen wall. Both of their desks had the same control over the colony. She had the better chair.

Romeo grabbed his drink bottle, leaning back in the chair after releasing the back to hit that ever-so-perfect 45-degree lean. It was comfortable, and the chair was close enough to the wall that he rested his head as he opened his canteen.

Water was a commodity at first. Rationing was the pits, but it was a necessary evil until they found the lake. However, after analyzing the water from Lake Westing, several hundred kilometers away, they determined they could distill out its oddness and have abundant pure water. Moreover, rainfall in that area was slightly higher than where they lived, so the lake's level never decreased after setting up a collection system that provided a consistent, clean water source with minimal filtration or distilling.

Suzanne Kel'er, the colony water treatment engineer, set up the facility with her counterpart from Mexico, Ricardo Aqua. Whom she calls Water Boy. She named the treatment facility 'Ko O Bi Omi' in her native tongue from Nigeria, Yoruba. No one questioned the name of the water treatment plant, and everyone got used to it. Needless to say, Suzanne had a sense of humor. In her native language, it translated to '**Clear as Mud**." The colony kept the name, and now they embrace it!

The lake contained a plethora of fish, and the settlement inhabitants sampled quite a few of the offerings. But, if you catch something unique, you have to name it. Then, cook and eat it once medical gives the green light. Your review would become the official review, flavor profile, and description in the database for that fish.

Most colonists brought fishing equipment, bows, arrows, and other essential survival items. Quite a few carried a Tenkara fishing rod, which had been famous in Japan hundreds of years earlier. Although Tenkara donated rods to each of the colonists, several enjoyed using them for fishing. Moreover, they are easily carried and used. The rod and tackle weigh only a few grams and are small and compact enough to fit in a pack. They are the perfect survival equipment item. Designed mainly for streams and small rivers, they can be used from the shoreline with some practice.

After a few months, they discovered the lake encompassed a vast area underground. So rather than transporting the water from the surface lake, they could tap into the underground lake a few kilometers from the colony. It was somewhat artesian, so pumping was unnecessary. In addition, the tap was quite a bit up in the mountains, so gravity brought the water to the plant between the two towns. They also discovered the water tapped near the colony was cleaner than the water in the lake, which meant faster distribution and less treatment was necessary. As a result, the entire colony area had hot and cold running water.

It was rather deep, but they had the equipment to create a water purification plant. It has been in operation for several years now. It produces enough water for the colony to not worry about water in the least. There are a few water towers that fill automatically when

"Computer, scan all frequencies," Romeo said. It was a standard command reiterated by Romeo or his boss occasionally throughout their shift, maybe every hour or so. He thought about setting up a secondary system to continuously monitor but has not gotten around to it yet.

The scan of all standard communications frequencies took precisely 4 minutes and 12 seconds. Romeo watched the clock tick down in the upper right corner of his screen, knowing that in 40 seconds, it would be completed, and he could resume watching the news live from Earth.

With 5 seconds remaining, the clock turned red, "….3, This is Colony Ship 3 calling anyone. This is a recorded message. We landed on a planet, but not the correct planet or star system, for that matter. We all survived the landing, including the animals, and have lived well here. It has been 29 months, Earth calendar, since landing, and the communications array became active only moments ago when we discovered the elements needed to make the repairs. There was minor damage that was finally repaired. Abundant natural food is available, and freshwater covers most of the world, so that is not an issue. We only need to contact Earth to let them know we are well. We are in the process of determining our exact location for you, but suffice it to say, we believe we have landed on the 4th planet in orbit of Ross 128. Larger than Earth, but with lush vegetation and abundant resources. Reminiscent of the Amazon basin before humanity raped it. We are tidally locked, and on the planet's dark side, so solar radiation is not an issue. The ambient temperature is comfortable and varies less than 3 degrees. We will be broadcasting this on frequency E1, Yellow channel, for as long as it takes to get a response. We will monitor E2, the Maroon channel, for any replies. This message repeats." There was a 5-second pause, "Colony Ship 3 calling any humans, this is Colony Ship 3 calling any humans from the planet Earth. We are well. We are alive, and we are surviving. Colony Ship 3, This is Colony Ship 3 calling anyone. This is a recorded message. We landed on a planet, but not the correct planet or star system."

Romeo cut the audio and let it continue to record. C3 is alive! He froze. This was monumental. "What the hell am I supposed to do?" He said to himself out loud. Again, he was frozen in time. He had a lot of friends on C3 and thought they were all gone. Now they are back. After hesitation, he tapped his desk and connected to his boss's comm in her home. She needed to confirm before they proceeded. That was protocol.

Wilomena Dumont appeared on the screen. He had woken her up, and she looked at the screen, "This had better be worth it." She said to him.

"I apologize for waking you; I know it was a long day. Let me play you something that just came in on a random frequency." There was a pause, and then she heard, "Colony Ship 3 calling any humans, this is Colony Ship 3 calling any humans from Earth. We are well. We are alive, and we are surviving. Colony Ship 3! This is Colony Ship 3 calling anyone. This is a recorded message. We landed on a planet, but not the correct planet or star system."

She was fully awake and excited, "Be there in 5 minutes." She disconnected the channel, and Romeo listened to the message repeatedly. He could not believe his ears.

4-minutes later, she walked into their office. Romeo relinquished the seat behind her desk. She sat, giving Romeo an evil glare as she locked her chair back so as not to tumble backward.

Wilomena tapped a few buttons and listened twice to the entire recorded message. Then, finally, she looked at him, "How did you find this?"

"I know. It's not a standard communications frequency. It's an emergency channel for the colony ships. The very low band is not a normal frequency range. I scan all possible frequencies when running a scan. DC to light, I call it. Takes just under 5 minutes. They must use ridiculous power to get it here with that power level. They're like 14 light-days from us. I looked up the location of Ross 128, which is quite a bit farther than I thought. So what the hell happened?" Romeo replied.

He looked at her, and she waited for him to answer her question, "Oh, I instructed the computer to scan all frequencies. It found this on the low-frequency emergency band."

"Well, Mr. Rodriguez, wake up the powers that be. You found them. You let people know." She paused, "In the meantime, I will attempt to establish communications with our brothers and sisters of Colony 3."

She turned the transmitter to the Maroon channel and spoke.

Realizing this was hard to keep a lid on, they never tried. Instead, Romeo set up a live broadcast of the conversation with Colony 3. Since it was on a priority channel in the first place, they woke up every household in the settlement, both towns, when their screens activated and the audio filled their homes.

Wilomena spoke, "Colony 3, this is Wilomena Dumont. As your repeating message stated, I am contacting you on the Maroon Emergency channel. I am from Colony Ship 1. We landed on the scheduled planet and have set up a thriving community. We number nearly 700 now since the incorporation of Colony Ship 2. The Data ARC is in full effect here. This conversation is transmitted to all screens in our colony and home to Earth in real time. We look forward to speaking to you and seeing you face to face one day."

Romeo just stood there and watched. He was still somewhat shocked that his periodic scan contacted fellow lost colonists.

He felt joy, excitement, and trepidation, but his friends were still alive.

CHAPTER TWO

Realizing this was hard to keep a lid on, Wilomena and Romeo did not even try. Therefore, the Earth was getting a live feed, more or less, and all homes and screens in Terra were getting the same video feed.

Wilomena spoke again, with the exact words but a bit more excitement, "Colony 3, this is Wilomena Dumont. I am from Colony Ship 1. We landed on the scheduled planet and have set up a thriving community. We number nearly 700 now since the incorporation of Colony Ship 2. The Data ARC is in full effect here, and this conversation is concurrently transmitted to Earth. We look forward to speaking to you and seeing you face to face one day."

There was a delay, but the voice of Colony 3 came in this time and was much clearer.

"Willy. I thought we would never talk again." The woman's voice was crystal clear and excited.

Wilomena recognized that name, "Only one person in this universe ever called me that; this has got to be Isabella Zee. Izzy! Are you running the HR section on that little rock?"

"Nope! They made me the Governor, but it was not my choice. They told me they appreciated my organizational skills, and I hope I did not disappoint them in the last 7 months. But hey, you have been there for 5 years now."

"Actually, I have been here for almost six years. We have a pretty good life here and hope to do some trading with you one day. I assume you ate your starship to build your settlement. You are the Governor?"

"We did, but we have a few propulsion engineers, a.k.a. rocket scientists, who tell me the shuttles they created can get to you in a few days. Maybe not the speed of light, but close. Besides, we have a ton of extra fruits and veggies we need to unload, and we need raw building materials for making metals. Iron, titanium, and similar. Copper and silver also, if possible. They are just about finished with the cargo shuttle, and we will take that to meet up with you." She took a breath, "As for me being Governor, well, we lost a few, quite a few actually, when we first landed."

"How long have you been dirt side?" Wilomena asked.

"We have been here a bit under three Earth years. It seems we bypassed a huge section of space and fell into a door or something into a new place. Lucky us."

"You what?" Wilomena exclaimed.

"The way I understand it, there was a rift in space, and because we were all sleeping and the computer had no idea what to make of it, we flew into it. We ended up a lot of lightyears from where we were supposed to be when we finally woke up. The computer realized we were not in the right place and found something close. After entering the system, we blasted Genesis to a promising planet, the only one in the system where we could breathe. We spent a few months in a parking orbit watching the weather and the planet; it all looked good in a few areas. Finally, we sent a team down, and they had a little campout for a month, and we woke everyone up and voted to stay."

"What's it like?"

"Higher gravity, rain forest, many critters, and a few are tasty. Abundant veggies and air and water. No pollutants, nothing that can kill you. So, a lot better than space, and not too bad in general."

"Izzy, our Governor wants to talk to you. We can catch up later. But wait, your shuttle can get here in a couple of days? How is that possible?"

"Did I mention we have a rocket scientist in the colony? You may have heard of him, Beeker. The guy who designed our ships, freeze tubes, and other things. He decided that the last available seat on our ship was for him. He installed his personal chair and popsicle tube, so how could we say no? He felt stagnant when we landed and decided to build a shuttle to check out the planet. Took him and his team a month, but got one that could see the entire surface quickly. We even plopped a couple of satellites in orbit to maintain vigilance in our new home and the surrounding space. As he calls it, his ***'light shuttle'*** is just about finished. I had no idea he was designing a light shuttle. Glad it ain't a heavy shuttle!" She laughed at her own joke.

"There is something wrong with you, still. In that case, we can have a drink when you get here." She paused, "But, first, find out if your communications team has your Data ARC set up. If so, I will link our system to your settlement, and you can piggyback on the data stream with Earth and call home!"

"Will do, Willy. Thanks." She paused a moment, "Who is your governor?"

A man walked over to the desk and occupied the seat as Wilomena stood. "Hi, Isabella. My name is Marcus Samuel."

"I remember you! Left-handed, and you like wider margins than most normal people." She was laughing as she said it.

Marcus laughed and said, "Guilty as charged. We have quite a few things going for us here, but a long growing season is not one of them. Plant-based food products will be appreciated. We found a titanium mine, well, not really a mine. An asteroid or something made of pure titanium crashed here long ago, and we use it to create new things, like vehicles and walls. We also made a pipe out of it to drill into the ground for fresh water. Our colony has hot and cold running water and an amazing solar power facility. Copper is here, but gold is more abundant. We have had an annoying number of weapons since the military was in Colony 3. Still, they shoehorned their guns in with our stuff by mistake."

"Well, Marcus, give us a couple of weeks, and we should be there to visit with you in person."

"Wait. You are several light days from us. You think you can get here in a few weeks?" Marcus paused a moment, then added, "Several light days. How are you? Are you several light days from us? We all launched in the same general direction."

"True. Dr. Beeker has a thought on that. It seems we hit an anomaly, a tunnel, or something. The nav logs have us in one place 13 years after launch, and we entered this system at the 29-year mark. Since no human was awake, we could only look at the logs. In less than 2 minutes, we traveled a lot of lightyears. Think of it as you will. I just call it the anomaly." She paused, "No, a few days is the trip we would need to take to get to you, but the week or two is how long we need to finish the shuttle prep and then a few days to load it up. We have already visited a few planets in this system and discovered many things we made use of; for example, a few hours from here, a small world developed these mean little creatures. They attack and try to kill and eat anything. Our marines had a field day with them, and they brought about 40 of them for examination. We did not want to slaughter our livestock since they were more valuable on the hoof than the spit. These creatures taste like beef and have many of the same nutrients, but the texture of the meat is similar to chicken. So I think the cows and the chickens sighed in relief when we found them."

"That sounds interesting. On your planet, are there any predators?" Marcus asked.

"None. Chipmunk size, mostly. We see a raccoon-sized thing occasionally, but we leave them all alone. Not worth the effort. We call the raccoon-size thing a Heythere because they get into everything and are the most curious creatures on the planet. They are not afraid of people and are mostly docile and playful. A few keep them as pets, and they usually act like cats. Yes, they house train perfectly."

"What do you call the terror thing from the nearby planet?"

“We call them a Devil Cat. About the size of an extra-large house cat but stricken with the devil. What?” She paused momentarily, speaking to someone else at her location, “Hang on a sec, Marcus.”

She was gone for a minute.

“Marcus, we should be arriving there on our landing day. We made landing day a holiday here, celebrating a community feast. Since about 30 of us will be with you, we will bring the feast. A sampling of the flavors of Rest Stop.”

“Rest Stop?”

“Yep, that’s what we called the planet. The settlement's name is Double Down, or DD for short.”

“Interesting name”

“Well, the settlement families got together and allowed each family to put a name in the hat for the town. Then, each family was allowed to vote for two names. Cutting the list in half. We did that a lot of times and ended up with three names. Double Down, Cougarville, and Newton were the top three. Newton was our gathering point before launch; Newton, North Carolina. We launched from the Outer Banks Spaceport as you did. We named the lake near us Lake Newton. Newton was a relaxing and peaceful place, and so was the lake with its name. Cougarville is our second settlement, about a 30-minute casual walk from the main settlement. Most of the businesses ended up being in Cougarville. I refer to that town as the Cougarville Emporium since you can spend the day shopping and lose yourself in the experience.” She paused momentarily, “The county seat, so to say, and where I reside is called Double

Down. Mostly administration, but also produce preservation. We have such a wide variety of produce. The cooks and canners took over a warehouse and preserved a lot of the produce in abundance. We just refer to it as the grocery store. If you need something, you just drop in and pick it up. People volunteer to help with canning as they have the time." She cleared her throat primarily for effect, "We have an established government like on Earth, but really scaled down for just a state, more or less."

"Your settlements have names? I like that! We call ours one and two. The lake we get the water from is Westing. Named after the guy who discovered that lake." Marcus said.

"A couple of our doctors are Victoria and Rebecca Westing." Izzy said, "Any relation?"

Romeo nodded to Marcus. "It seems that they are. Romeo here knows them, it appears, and is bobbing his head up and down like a kid's toy."

"Romeo, you mean Romeo Rodriguez?"

"That's him."

"Nice."

"You two know each other?"

"In a way." She replied and changed the subject. Everyone noticed and smiled. Wilomena remembered they were a thing at the training center during survival training. They paired up for their month in the mountains. She smiled at Romeo, and he winked back at his boss. Wilomena and Romeo talked about her a few years ago. They 'had a thing' for 6 months at the Youngsville training center. It was getting pretty serious, and then the ship assignments came out. He was on ship 2, and she was on ship 3. They were falling in love, but it would be a long time till they could be together. So they broke it off but remained friends, good friends at that.

During the exchange, Izzy kept saying, “Roger Beeker is looking to speak to your scientist, but he wants to do it in person. He also has plans for the lightship and thinks you can build one. I do not understand the process, but it uses a near-light speed travel ship thingy and opens the door to another location, a new point in space. He said the doors need to be well away from a solar system, so we travel a few days, open the door, fly through, and travel a few days. Then we can establish a trade route between us.” Then, she spoke to someone at her location, “According to Roger, the trip to Earth would be a little over a month. A lot different than 30 years. I find it amazing that Earth has not been out here yet.”

“I know. In three decades, they have not approached the light barrier in propulsion. But there is a good reason. Brace yourself, Izzy.” He paused for her to realize this was not good news, “Yellowstone erupted and put the planet into a nuclear winter a year after you launched. All technology and inventions went into surviving the cold and the dark. Maybe we can help them somehow, like send the plans to Earth and let them build the ship and come visit.”

“Great idea.” She paused a moment, “How many survived?”

“Roughly one-third of Earth perished initially. The initial explosion removed a multi-state chunk of North America and all its residents. They recovered in a couple of years and created a safe place on the surface. The blast sent dust, dirt, rocks, and stuff into orbit with the initial explosion. There is a dust ring around the planet now. Saw pictures from the lowest station, and it really looks odd. No longer the blue marble, more like a brown and gray rock. The cleanup of the planet included low orbit. Still, thankfully, within a decade, most of the debris in space had returned to the surface. The stations and the lunar colony were on their own for a few years. A couple of the stations converted cargo holds to food production. Once the transports could get into space again, the food was welcomed. I understand they reserved one large cargo area for use as cold storage. All they did was vent it to space. They managed to stockpile a lot of food before the shuttle service resumed, and Earth welcomed it openly."

"Is Earth doing OK now?" She asked.

"OK is a relative term, but let's just say they are much better. After three decades, they know what can and needs to be done to accomplish a goal and just do it."

There was a silent pause as she contemplated the fate of her homeworld, then in a new chipper voice, "I never asked. What time is it there?"

"Time? Ah! Our little planet has a 22-hour day and a 360-day year. So we use an 11-hour shift, with a 60 to 90-minute lunch. Currently, the time is 5:12 am. How about you?"

"Our year is a bit longer, but the day is about the same."

"I guess that means gravity is a bit higher there?"

"Yes, it is. Took a while to get used to it, but most have adapted well. Unfortunately, we lost quite a few colonists due to gravity sickness. That is what we call it. Sadly, a few are worse off because of the higher gravity. We may bring them with us on the trip to visit in hopes they will get better. Perhaps they can move there if their symptoms go into remission." She paused to contemplate her next statement, "We lost a third of our population in the first few weeks. Strokes and heart issues were primarily due to increased gravity, increased work the body had to do just to breathe, and blood pressure issues when you stood up. People passed out quickly, and we got used to that happening. A sad thing to get used to in reality."

"Feel free to bring your people here to see if they recover. They would be welcome to stay if they want."

Izzy said, "I was just informed that the ARC antenna is set and ready for the relay."

Romeo said into the transmitter, "Excellent! Since BLUE is a clear channel here and there. Can you open the blue channel, and we can run the ARC to you on blue?"

Another voice from Colony 3, "ARC set to blue. Receiving at minus forty Db."

"Increasing power, let me know as it attains nominal," Romeo said.

"Increasing, minus fifteen.... Minus ten.... Power level at zero. Perfect! Setting return signal at similar."

"We are receiving you at minus three. You can leave it there for now. Opening data ARC routing." Then, a few seconds later, "OK, you are on the ARC!"

"Fast data test, please," Romeo asked.

They ran a data through-put test from both ends individually, "A little low, 42 quad. But considering the distance, I think it will suffice."

Romeo replied, "Same here, 41 quad. That is well inside the green. You should have full functionality." He paused, "Sending you the Earth and Terra phonebook."

It was an antiquated term, but understood. Back home, there were codes to contact specific people, departments, and places; now, they know who is who. All are accessed through the data interface.

"OK," Wilomena took over, "Let's cut this and reconnect later through the ARC. Then, it should be clearer, at least, no static."

"Understood. Rest Stop signing off. THANKS, WILLIE!!"

The channel died off, and people left her office. Once her office emptied, she picked up the paper and looked at Romeo.

He responded, "Oh, in all that fun and excitement, I forgot to mention. It looks like someone is stealing. I watched several shed vids over the past few weeks. Someone entered the building several times and removed items when the building was secured and locked up."

"Who did you see?" She asked. "What was taken?"

“Not 100% certain at this point, but let me check, and I will let you know what I find in the next few days. I would hate to give you a name and be wrong.” He paused, “As for what they borrowed, seemingly permanently, construction tools mostly from the shed. They were also borrowing items from the mess and maintenance.”

“To what end?” Wilomena asked.

“No clue, a guess. They plan to start their own town somewhere. So, everything they steal is needed to start a community. But the thing is, there is no place to store hidden items anywhere in the colony. So what are they doing with them? I’ll have an off-the-record chat with the Handies. If anyone on the planet has heard anything, even a rumor, it would be them. They see and hear and are essentially invisible.” Romeo said.

“Talk to the Colonel first, please. I heard that the Handies and her have a working relationship.” Willie said.

“Interesting. The eyes of the colony?”

“Something like that.” Wilomena thought a moment as the door opened, “OK. Please talk with Colonel Dryer about this. She is colony security, after all. They may have run into a stash of tools and not realized what they were looking at.”

“Will do!” He winked and nodded his head.

Marcus Samuel entered the room. “So…..”

“What?” She replied.

“What do you make of this?’

She looked at him. He sounded suspicious of Izzy, but she said things only Izzy would know. "I think it's great. We're getting tourists in a few weeks!"

CHAPTER THREE

Over the past few weeks, Colony 1 completed the barracks they started several months ago to give singles a place to live as they come of age. With the arrival of 30+ visitors from Colony 3, Rest Stop, the barracks have been renamed Nina Hotel. Initially, this would be used by unmarried young people as they attain the age to get a job or take a trade. Two floors of efficiency apartments on the second and third floors are designed for singles mainly or new couples. The first floor contains two and three-bedroom suites.

Upper floors, 18 units total. Each has a large bed, facilities, a living area, and a kitchenette. The lower floor is similar to a two or three-bedroom apartment design. Each bedroom has facilities, a common living area, and a kitchen.

With 18 units on the upper floors and 8 units on the first floor (4-2 bedroom units and 4-3 Bedroom units), quite a number of people, 50 single people, can reside in this facility. Since all beds in the building are queen and king size, if every room was a couple, the residents would total 100. There are 8 more of these structures planned in the central colony and more in the works in the second colony. Sets of friends are already hoping to gain residence in the 3-bedroom suites.

In the other town area, the construction of the Pinta Hotel should be completed in a month. Also has 3 floors, but this structure is an 'L' shape, with a similar layout to the original Nina Hotel doubled in each wing. The first floor of one structure is a club. A bar, a hangout, a restaurant. A fellowship and gathering place. They even constructed the bow of a ship, dubbed the Pinta, behind the bar. Since there is no real money here, payment is accomplished in trade.

Marcus decided the planet's name was Terra, not the settlement, and asked for suggestions. They had two distinct locations, ship one landing zone and ship 2 landing zones.

Ship one area, which encompasses both towns, has been dubbed Centauri to commemorate their system for easy identification, like a county or possibly the first state on the planet. The central community, or the ship one community area, has been named Columbus after the prime pilot of their three well-known historical watercraft.

The second community was allowed to name its town. They called it New Sydney since most of the population hailed from Australia.

Wilomena added the new area code for Rest Stop to the dialing program on her shift. She connected the communication array through the ARC to Rest Stop. Pulled the comm codes and names for the entire colony and made them available. In the first couple of weeks, the ARC was very busy. Calls to Earth, calls to Rest Stop, calls just to say hello and chat. It was terrific as old friends reconnected and family on Earth discovered their long-lost relatives survived. It was a happy and joyous time for all three communities of humanity.

Marsha Cassellari, the lead vet on ship 1, and Michael Ramon, the lead vet on ship 2, called Maria, Marsha's twin sister, who was the lead vet on ship 3. Classmates, friends, and now in-laws. She was excited for them and happy they, as she said, FINALLY found each other. She introduced them to her husband, Kevin Lancaster. Kevin is the lead vet tech under Maria, studying to be a full veterinarian. All three vets ensured they brought books and training materials to continue the profession and train others in their careers.

As the people of Rest Stop read the news and watched the vid, they learned about Earth, the eruption, the new technologies, and the redirection of science from the future to the present, from learning new things to helping humanity survive.

Wilbur Jacks was sitting at the console as the most current news feed arrived. He watched the announcer talk about particulate matter, sulfur levels, and other toxins.

Terra was used to this report each day, but he was not. Over the past few weeks, he and Romeo have talked quite a bit. They worked the same shift, more or less. The gravity was higher since they had a 22-hour day but a slightly faster rotation on a much larger planet. That was an important topic. How can a mere human survive and adapt to that environment?

Wilbur did an experiment one morning shortly after he arrived and could move freely. He had a scale, went to the workout area, and pulled a one-kilogram weight. He knew this plate weighed one kilogram in Earth's normal gravity, and when he placed it on the scale, it weighed one point six kilograms. Therefore, if you weighed 100 kilos, you carried around 160 kilos.

They decided to recalibrate all the scales in the settlements except a few. So, if you stood on the scale, you knew your weight as it would be on Earth.

Romeo mentioned that the gravity on Terra was .8 that of Earth, so when those from Rest Stop arrived, they may have coordination issues since their muscles are so used to working harder for the same result. Opposite for anyone visiting Rest Stop from Terra.

Romeo's desk rang. "Don't even need to look who's calling me. Howdy, Will. What's up?"

"Not much. Have all of you accepted the fact Earth is trashed?"

Rameo shook his head, "Pretty much. Nothing we can do from here, so we just accept it and move on. A few have not had the greatest of times because of the event, but we are all past it for the most part. It took a while, so you must give it some time. When ship two arrived, all of us relived the horror of it all like it was the first time, and some of us relived it all again as Rest Stop got the information. I just accept it and move on. Nothing I can do from here anyway."

"I have been looking for what they are talking about when they talk about the pit. What is that?"

"Well, the hole created when the caldera exploded threw up tons and tons of material. I'm talking about the topsoil from the crust, magma, and lithosphere, and they think it went as deep as the upper to the main mantle. That means that the hole was at least 80 kilometers deep. It took a decade to cool enough to get to it. Still, once they did, they tossed a GPS drone into it. They let it drop as far as possible, eventually stopping at 72 kilometers. They tried to get it to return, but the poor thing stopped transmitting a few minutes later. You can find the video of it if you search for the Yosemite video drone. I watched it for about an hour, and it looked pretty scary. I cannot believe anyone would want to voluntarily drop into the pit."

"So, something like why would anyone strap into a rocket and fly asleep for three decades to find a new world, hopefully?"

Romeo smiled, "Yeah, something like that." Then, he changed the subject, "Anyone there making any adult beverages you can bring for us, I mean me, to sample?"

"As a matter of fact, yes. A plant here; it looks like an odd cactus but tastes like a mango. It makes an exquisite tequila-type beverage. That is by far my favorite. Others use standard veggies and make vodka or whiskey, but I like the local hooch personally."

"Here, we found this thing that looks like a pastel purple potato. It's the size of giant yams and makes the most interesting vodka-ish type of drink. I mix it with coffee into a sorta like coffee liquor. I was always partial to White Russians in my 20s, which is reasonably close. I had a few cases of it, but it looks like someone borrowed a couple of the cases last night." Romeo pulled himself from his reverie, "The taste is rather unique, but hey, so is sake!"

"Good point. Took me a while till I liked the taste of sake, but before I left home, I found a few bottles, cases actually, to put into my personal stash. The stuff is nearly forty years old and is REALLY good. So I'll bring one, and you can try it out."

"Thanks. Been a long time since I had sake." He paused, "So, I hear thirty of you coming to visit. Any idea who that may be?"

"Actually, yes. I have the manifest right here. Since there are 30 seats on the ship, someone fills each seat. Governor, Mayor, Comm Lead, me, Beeker, programmer, electronics, medical, Vet Services, military, and about a dozen people suffering from gravity sickness." He grinned, "That's what we are calling it."

"That's not 30. So why are they sending a Veterinarian? So I take it a few are the crew. OH, by the way, I wonder something." He paused briefly, "I am curious how high you can jump now?"

"No clue. It may be fun, though." He changed the subject, "You are correct; Beeker and the ship's crew are not included in the 30. But the last 10 or so are a lottery. Put your name in a hat, and you will get to go visit the other colony. My wife wants to visit, a vacation, I guess. Actually, I think she wants to keep an eye on me. Her name is in the hat as well. The vet is to tell your vet about our animals, local critters, and the cat."

"So, an 8-day trip, with 30 of your closest friends, in a tin can. Sounds like a plan. Is there a shower on the ship?"

"Damn, no clue. I hope so. If not, you may kick us off the planet when the door opens." They both laughed.

Wilomena walked in and looked at the wall. "Hi Will, How's life in the jungle?"

Another voice replied to her question. "Me, Tarzan, you, Jane." William Mew, Wilbur's boss, walked in about the exact moment as Wilomena.

"Hi, Bill." She said, "Now, serious question. Is there anything you need relating to communications that we can prepare for you? Then, of course, we had the tech-heavy ships with 1 and 2."

"Actually, do you have a few spare portable radios we can get from you? I can reprogram them as needed, but we can use 25 more. When we landed, the impressive gravity popped a strap, and the corner of a large, heavy container of cattle feed landed on the box of spare radios. They are a pile of spare parts now. Also, if you have a repeater until ours is finished. Doc is making one out of old hunks of the colony ship that is in pieces in storage."

Romeo spoke, "I will look around. I know of maybe 1 or 2 radio storage boxes we have not touched yet. Since everyone was issued a radio at launch and few failed, we still have all our spares available. They are still in the container they were shipped in, so you can have those; as for the repeater, it's funny you should ask. I just finished putting one together. We planned to put it at the lake, but it would not transmit a hundred kilometers, so that was scrapped. You can rent that one for a while. I do have another spare."

"What's the range?" Will laughed, "Rent?"

"At 12 watts off your handy talkie, you should get maybe 30 kilometers around the repeater if the repeater antenna is at least 10 or 20 meters off the ground. The repeater is 200 watts; if the antenna is high enough, it may have a 300-kilometer coverage area. It is a digital repeater, so it is crystal clear. If you can hit the system, it will do you right."

"Perfect. I'll take it. Did you set it to the 6-meter band? We rekeyed all our radios to 6."

"Yep. Sure did. The lower frequency is needed as far as the current comm is concerned. I used 50.125 MHz."

At the same time, they said, "The magic band!" They laughed, and their bosses shook their heads. Being radio operators and communications specialists, they all understood the reference to the 6-meter band.

An amateur radio set of frequencies that both acts like you expect it to perform and does fantastic things it is not supposed to do when it gets a wild hair. Distances did not really matter if the conditions were right. These two planets have an active ionosphere, so 6 meters was chosen for clarity and range. Of course, the fact it was a digital communications system made it all that much clearer.

"It's odd. Like a sporadic E reflection on this planet, the effect is nearly year-round and not all that sporadic. We have talked almost a thousand kilometers from HT to HT, which is intermittent at best.

"Hey Will, I was thinking….." Romeo said.

"Did it hurt?" Will replied very quickly.

"Not too bad…." Romeo said back to him on a reflex.

Will continued, "You were thinking about setting up a cross-band repeater at the lake and one near the colony."

"Yup. When you are here, you wanna check out the lake. There is a small hill on the front side. We can set up the repeater and put its opposite number on the hill in my backyard, maybe half a klick from the settlement."

"Sounds like fun, actually."

"Perfect, we can head out for a few days after you get here and let our bosses be bossy."

Bill and Wilomena shook their heads and looked at Romeo and Wilbur. Bill said, "Then, if you get it to work on Terra, you can set something like that up here."

"I guess I need to go to Rest Stop to help Will?" Romeo said.

"Please remember that gravity is about 50% more on Rest Stop." Bill said, "You may have some issues when you arrive."

"I know, I ain't forgotten," Romeo said, looking at his boss and winking. She shook her head.

William continued, "OK, I guess an eyeball QSO in a couple of weeks."

"73, brother," Romeo replied, and their bosses just stared at them.

~~~~~~~~~~~
~~~~~~~~~~~

"…..they should be here tomorrow sometime," Marcus said to the comm system.

"Great! I am sending you a questionnaire you can give to them. The same one you filled out when you went online. I am hoping they can finish it before they depart. Any idea how long they plan to stay on Terra?"

"Not a clue. But I hear the plans for the light shuttle are pretty easy, and we plan to build one in the next few months. We are building a spaceport and have finished the landing strip, and the hanger was started yesterday. Have you had the plans reviewed?"

"We all looked at them. Nice system, and we will be building a small fleet next year. It is a basic craft but has a few bells and whistles. If for nothing else, they would be much better than what we currently use for intersystem cargo runs. "

"I know, right? But, if it has bells and whistles, it must have glitter to be done right!"

"I do agree." They both laughed a moment.

Marcus Samuel was alone in his office on the other side of the colony for the moment. His office had a large window facing the hills surrounding the settlement on three sides, protecting it from weather and storms. That view was directly behind him and entirely on screen as he was talking to his boss on Earth.

"One day, I hope to be there and see that view in person."

"Is gold still expensive on Earth?" Marcus asked.

“Not so much, really. Since they found the universe's gold vault in the asteroid belt and brought back more gold than was on the entire planet, there is a search for a new currency backing. Several currencies are experimenting with platinum and other precious metals. It does, however, still make good jewelry. Although credits are used, trade is a bigger compensation for nearly everything. So why do you ask?”

“On the floor next to my desk is a paperweight. A solid gold rock. 18 kilograms in weight. I can send you one?”

“Wow, that’s cool! I would love that on my desk.” He laughed a little more, “Just think, that thing would be worth a million credits… I mean a few million dollars for my great-great-grandfather.”

“I’ll send you one.” His face changed, “Now, we need to get down to business. When the shuttles are active, what can we send you? How can we help Earth?”

“We have had to put a halt or a slow down on all ore processing because of the atmosphere and the dust layer. So, any refined ore would be perfect. If you can create a giant dust filter and clean Earth, that would be great!”

“I’ll have my teams get right on that,” Marcus said jokingly.

~~~~~~~~~~~

“This is a cargo shuttle Pluto on approach to Terra. You ready for us yet?”

“Well, unless you want to hang in orbit a few days, come on down. I hear you all need a shower anyway.”
~~~~~~~~~~~

“That is a fact!” He was silent for a heartbeat, “I see us at atmospheric impact in 12 minutes with wheels down 6 minutes later.”

“We set up a beacon. It will lead you to the end of the runway. The landing strip is two kilometers long. Is that long enough?” Beacons are set to a standard frequency and low power.

“We only need 50 meters.”

They dropped through the atmosphere, and a boom could be heard.

Romeo looked around the area and noticed a man wearing a black pullover jacket with a hood. It seems like the jacket he saw on the vids from the shed and a few other places he found on the security cameras.

He approached the person whose face was concealed at the moment and stopped in front of him. He turned around, apparently too fast, and ran into him. He looked at his face and recognized him, apologizing for bumping into him. Romeo walked off to meet someone; bumping into him was an accident.

Romeo headed for the landing zone.

The man got nervous when Romeo bumped into him; it did not seem random. Why would he be in the crowd?

Dayl Warrin quietly left the area by a back route. He thought he had been discovered. OK then, he may need to advance his timetable.

CHAPTER FOUR

"Shuttle Pluto, you are clear to land. Follow the beacon."

"Affirmative Terra Control. We are 4 minutes from wheels down."

The entire inhabitants of Terra were gathered, lined up, crowding around the newly created landing area. Nearly a thousand people lined the runway, the street, and the crowded area near the landing zone.

Although it was a two-kilometer landing strip, it had a landing spot for craft that are vertical take-off and landing capable, of which the shuttle Pluto is one.

A sonic boom erupted from the sky, and everyone looked in that direction. Allison Rainer pointed to a spot in the sky somewhat north of where most were looking, and everyone was tracking the shuttle. Unfortunately, it was still too far to see any detail. It was just a tiny black dot against the perfect blue. The visitors had perfect weather today, just another perk for a great event.

It passed over the colony a minute later, and they got a perfect look at it. It is squarer than what they imagined but at the same time beautiful. One description was geometric synchronicity.

The engines were fore and aft, port and starboard on the bottom, obviously for orbital maneuvering and hovering, which means vertical landing and take-off. There is a set of thrusters on the rear. Two above and two below what looks like a cargo hatch. The underside engines were flush with the skin, and the rear engines were shaped like a rectangle exhaust port with soft corners.

Romeo stood beside the Colonel, "Sarah, you need your team to watch this shuttle. It seems I can prove there is a thief in the colony. I would hate for something of theirs to go missing."

"Theory or fact? Suspects?" She replied.

"It is on the fact side of theory at the moment, but the facts are starting to rapidly line up. I will know for sure in the next few days. As for the suspect, I have one. I plan to follow him this evening and see where he goes because all the stuff he takes has got to be hidden somewhere in the hills."

"Be careful, please. You got me on comms if you need backup." She said, and she started to walk away, closer to the shuttle. Romeo followed.

The shuttle touched down softly, engines went silent, and the rear cargo hatch slowly lowered, opening from the top and becoming a ramp.

The day was perfect. The temperature is 23°C with no clouds in the sky. A soft plume of dust settled as the shuttle touched down. The cargo door opened from the top and lowered to the ground, becoming a ramp leading into the craft's cargo bay.

The anticipation in the waiting crowd was palpable. The anxiety could be felt clearly. Then, finally, the Governor, Izzy, Isabella Zee, appeared in the cargo doorway, and the assembled crowd went nuts.

A moment later, the doorway was filled with people. Some are supported by others. The colonists who suffered from gravity sickness. Izzy walked down the ramp to the waiting reception team.

Marcus Samuel and his family; Tonya and her family; Wilomena and Romeo; Michelle Rowes – the lead scientist; Radika Metalia and the Wilkes – CMO; and Lieutenant Colonel Sarah Dryer – Security Chief.

“We made it!” Izzy yelled, and the crowd cheered again. “Take me to your leader!” Everyone laughed. A few moments later, the sound died off, and Marcus spoke.

“On behalf of Terra, I welcome you and your party to our little corner of the universe. As our first visitors, we thought it would be a good idea to officially name Rest Stop Landing Day today. So it’s an official holiday.”

There goes that crowd again.

Izzy introduced her team. “Governor, I am Isabela Zee. This is Roberto Mars, our Mayor or, more accurately, my #2. Bill Mew and Wilbur Jacks are the comms here. You all know Roger Beeker, I’m sure. My CMO Rosa Martinez and my Chief of Security….” She was cut off by the woman standing next to Marcus.

“Major Droid!” said Lieutenant Colonel Sarah Dryer, who puffed up her chest like she wanted to fight.

"Dryer….. an interesting name. Do you wash, too?" Droid said as if it was a challenge. Slowly, they walked toward each other, and everyone just stared. Then they grabbed each other in a bear hug.

Izzy managed to open her mouth after that and speak. "I take it you two know each other."

The Major spoke, "Yes, Governor. The Colonel and I know each other quite well. At the academy, I had her as my instructor for multiple classes and my first assignment as a butter bar under her guidance."

Sarah looked at the two Gunnery Sergeants near her. "She any good?" Both of them nodded. "Good! If not, I may need to kick her ass from here to Earth." Both Gunnery Sergeants laughed a bit.

The Major looked at the new crowd, "I am Major Andrea Battle, but everyone calls me Droid."

Tonya asked, "Why Droid?"

The military types all grinned, "Well, Ma'am, when I was in OCS taking space ops, the Colonel here was a Major, my instructor, and a rather well-barbed thorn in my side."

She looked at the Colonel, who had that look on her face, then added, "But in a good way!" Everyone laughed.

She continued, "We had a real emergency during the training mission. The shuttle's computer system shut down, which meant we had maybe an hour of air. No one on the mission had a clue about repairing the computer system. Since it was dead, communication was also dead, so we could not ask for assistance. I stood and went to the data vault, and in 42 minutes, we were back online. My fellow cadets joked that I interfaced with the ship systems and repaired them from the inside, and it evolved to me being part android, and as it would appear, Droid stuck."

Willie Waynor, the Colony 1 electronics lead, asked, "How did you know what to do?"

The Major replied, "Well, funny that. I was in college for 3 years before I figured out what I wanted for a major…. My name at the time was Andrea Majors."

The Colonel added, "That would be the Major of Major Major's, right?" everyone laughed.

"Correct! I spent 3 years in computer security and electronics, then decided I wanted my new major to be Management Information Systems focusing on leadership and psychology."

"After three years, you changed your major? I bet your parents were happy about that!" The Colonel said.

The Major introduced the two security types to her former instructor. "Colonel, it is my greatest pleasure to introduce Gunnery Sergeant Brenda Battle and Gunnery Sergeant Kathy Battle." She winked at the Colonel, "My parental units!"

Sarah did a double-take, "Really?"

"Yes, ma'am, Gunny B is hand to hand and explosives, and Gunny K is strategics and training."

"Well, I guess the corp really is family!"

"So, what do you call them?" The Colonel asked.

Major Droid, as she is called, replied. Then, looking at Gunny Kathy, "This amazing woman I call Gunny K," Looking at the other, "And this amazing woman I call Brendar the Barbarian or simply Gunny B."

All who heard laughed. Gunny B just shook her head while Gunny K grinned from ear to ear.

Gunny B spoke, "If she wants to change her classes, that's on her. We gave her what we had saved for her schooling. When we did, we told her that the bank was closed. I understand that she took half and used it, invested the rest, and never had to work while in school. So, it all worked out!"

Izzy spoke. "OK, all. Let's get this show on the road. First things first, our sick and ill from the gravity, where can we put them?"

The CMO of the colony took over the conversation, "I am Dr. Helena Wilke, the CMO. We have a ten-bed facility, but we can easily double that, so…." She motioned to a few people off in the distance. "This is Dr. Radika Metalia, our lead researcher, educator, and all-around amazing woman." She smiled for a very brief moment.

The nurses and attendants approached and put them on gurneys, wheelchairs, and stretchers and brought them to the medical facility. Twenty-one of them in total. Additional beds were already being set up.

"I am the CMO from Rest Stop, Dr. Martinez. Call me Rosa, please. How can we assist? I have a few of my medical team with me. First, this amazing woman is Cathy Jacks. She was and is an OR nurse with another talent; she has an advanced degree she claims was just for fun. She is a research biologist and knows more about this illness than anyone."

"Call me Radika. Come along, doc. We can use you and your team." So, the Terra medical team headed for the hospital, a few minutes away. Once they all left, security spoke.

"So, we hear you have a lot of extra guns?" Gunny B asked.

The Colonel replied, "We do. Gunny's, all four of you, head to the armory and see what we have that you need. You know, go do Gunny stuff. Afterward, meet us at the barracks." She paused a moment, "This is Gunny Szell and Gunny Grimek. They are your counterparts. You four head that way, and the Major and I will meet up with you in a bit. We have some things to discuss."

The four military top enlisted headed off in another direction. Once they were a dozen steps away, "Droid, come with me to my office."

They left, and the others made small talk to one side while the military conversed.

Marcus raised his volume. "OK, let's head to the civic building." He turned and pointed to the science types. "These are our science teams. Can you all find a place to meet and discuss the scientific stuff?"

"We can, Marcus," Michelle said, introducing her science teams. They all began pairing off as they found their counterparts. Those who did not just fell in and fit in as needed.

The five from each side headed to the civic building. Leaders, administrators, and the communications teams. Time to do some strategic planning. As they walked, Wilbur and Romeo talked.

“Did your wife make the lottery?” Romeo asked.

“She did, more or less. She is not in the lottery but with the medical team. They needed her since she is the most knowledgeable about gravity illness.”

“Researcher?”

“Not really. She is an OR nurse by training, but not much Operating Room time is needed, so she stepped into a research role. Chemical and Biology degree. Masters in research biology, and when we left, she was really close to a doctorate in research biology. So, the CMO gave her a department; their first task was understanding the gravity illness. So she and the rest of the team focused on the gravity sickness.”

“Oh, she’s the amazing woman your CMO mentioned?” Romeo smiled.

“Yep. She is amazing.”

“What is it with the gravity?” Wilomena asked.

“Well, from what I hear, some people have a bad time adjusting to the higher gravity. Granted, we lost quite a few to gravity the first month on the surface, like a third of our population. It has finally tapered off, but we may lose someone in a week. Excessive stress on the body is fine for some of us, but for others, it really sucks. Heart problems, mostly. But the majority of us were able to adapt. We got stronger each day, and then, little by little, we could do things, and now, most of us can do whatever we need to do. Exertion may wind or tire us, but we do OK."

He paused momentarily, "Sad to say, it would take you a few months to get accustomed to the higher gravity if you visited us. Not worth the time if you come back here in the light G zone." He looked at the others, "You all understand. Everything we create here must support the weight as if it is 60% heavier. That has been the trick we finally figured out. As for people, you would be one hurting puppy when you landed at Rest Stop. Walking would be a chore. But, hell, standing would be an accomplishment."

"So, when you go to the Devil Cat planet…." Romeo's voice trailed off.

"We feel Super Human. It has gravity close to Earth's Moon. That's why none of our team was injured. The sheer strength and great weapons helped us survive when we arrived and were first attacked. Several of the team jumped straight up thirty meters into a tree."

~~~~~~~~~~

The tour of the central part of town concluded, and they met near the barracks. The gaggle of Gunny's appeared and joined the party.

Droid asked, "Find anything interesting?"

"Yes, Ma'am. We grabbed about 35% of the weapons, a few cases of stun and plasma grenades, maybe 25% of the reserve ammo, and a few shoulder-launched rockets."

Marcus looked at the Colonel, "We good?"
~~~~~~~~~~

“That is fine. We’ll never use all that anyway. If you need a few more, let me know.”

They walked toward the offices to coordinate the next few day’s activities. Chatting about nothing, in particular, all the way there. They directed their guests to the new barracks building as they arrived at the office. After a short time, they each had their room assignments.

The Mayor spoke, “What say we forego the planning today and allow you all to rehumanize? Shower, rest, food, and beverages.” He pointed to a small building they could all see, “That, my friends, is the First Bar and Grill. The beer is fresh and cold, and there is also a good selection of wines. Food, well, it’s bar food. Let’s meet there in 6 hours for dinner and a drink or three.”

The Major asked, “You are rather informal around here?”

“Yes, Droid, we are. We like it that way. It works perfectly for us.”

Major Droid instantly thought she said something wrong, “Colonel, I apologize. I meant nothing by the comment.”

“Not a problem, Major. Push it out of your mind.”

“Yes, Ma’am, but we are rather informal on Rest Stop. I like this place, the people, the attitude. Reminds me of home!” She smiled at them, “As in Rest Stop.”

The Governor, Marcus, spoke. “If I don’t get to the bar later, I will see you all in the morning at breakfast. Then, please take the rest of the day and, well, rest. Feel free to walk around, visit people and shops, and enjoy the sights.

Cougarville is that way; down that path, maybe 20 minutes walk. Lots of shops and artists."

Major Droid looked at the building next to, which had a two-story flat roof. An evil grin passed across her face; her parents shook their heads in sync, and everyone noticed. She squatted down, almost sitting, and jumped.

"Holy crap!" Marcus said.

The Colonel yelled, "What exactly are you doing?"

She yelled down from the roof. "Testing a theory."

The Gunnies mumbled under their breath.

Gunny K said, "Oh my god, she is SO your daughter!"

Gunny B replied, "Mine, she is just as impulsive as you. I would have picked a lower roof to jump onto as my experiment."

"Not experiment, she said theory," Gunny K added.

"Oh, now that makes it all the better." Gunny B said.

At that moment, the Major landed next to her parents. Major Droid looked at them. They were still mumbling. The rest of the party just smiled and watched. Romeo was almost laughing.

"PARENTAL UNITS!" Droid said.

They stopped and froze.

"Sorry." They said together.

Gunny B added, "We sometimes ramble. Been together a long time, set in our ways."

Marcus broke the chain, laughing at the sight, "So, I guess the people of Rest Stop can do more things than the standard human."

The Major replied, "Guess so." Then, she approached a land vehicle, grabbed the rear end, and lifted it. It took some effort, but she lifted it. "Yup, guess so."

Marcus added, "If I get a flat tire, I know who to call if I can't find the jack." Everyone smiled or laughed momentarily, then Marcus said, "Well, have a good evening. Don't break anything. The dining hall is that building over there. If we don't meet at the bar in a few hours, we'll see you all in the morning." He looked toward the setting sun; on this planet, it gets dark fast when it sets. "Sunrise is in about 11 hours. We will convene about an hour after that for breakfast. You have everything you need in your rooms." He shook hands with the visitors.

As he turned and left, the visitors from Rest Stop all jumped onto the roof. They had a lot of fun. Marcus and the others with him turned slightly and looked as they walked, "That really looks like fun." Romeo said.

Major Droid yelled, "See you all at breakfast!"

The group turned and waved. This just may turn out to be a good working relationship.

Romeo returned to his office and opened a few camera feeds. He found his suspect, Dayl Warrin, on the video, and he was heading out of town and into the hills. Romeo hurriedly left his office and sprinted the kilometer to the last place he saw Dayl. He stopped and looked around, then heard a sound, footfalls, up in the hills above him. He followed the sound as quietly as possible for nearly an hour until he came up to where he stopped.

Climbing a few meters and pulling himself over a rock formation, he sat there, waiting. Finally, about 45 minutes later, he heard someone leaving and returning the way they had come.

He waited a little longer, and with today's winds, sounds could be muffled, so he looked. All clear.

He dropped back to the path and headed up that way. He saw a series of rocks that looked out of place and removed a few. Then, he found all the missing tools and stuff they didn't know about. He also found weapons.

He replaced the rocks to make it appear untouched and headed home. He returned via an alternate route from an antenna array nearby, in case he was seen in the hills; it made for a great cover story.

He removed his comm from his pocket as he walked, "Romeo to the Colonel."

"Go ahead, Romeo."

"Bingo." He said into the comm, which was an unsecured communications system. "The test has run successfully. Meet me at my office, and we can review."

"How does an hour sound?"

"Perfect. See you then."

He cleared the frequency, put the HT back on his belt, and headed directly to his office.

Marcus, Wilomena, Colonel Sarah, and a few marines were waiting for him when he arrived.

Sarah looked at him as he entered, "We need to talk."

Marcus continued, "Tell us everything you know, and the Colonel and her team will continue the investigation."

"OK, but I got him dead to rights. I know where he is stashing the stolen items, including weapons. So let me start at the beginning."

Romeo told them the story, what he found, and where.

CHAPTER FIVE

“Good morning,” Marcus said as he entered the dining facility. He saw the manager, and she noticed him and approached.

“Marcus, I think that chow hall, dining hall, and dining facility are too boring, and I would like to give it a real restaurant name.”

Marcus stopped in his tracks. He had been thinking that same thing the night before as he was dozing off. Talking to the manager reminded him of the thoughts.

“Evelyn, I think that is a great idea. Since we will start having visitors soon, I think it is only fitting we christen our first restaurant. Come up with a name, a theme, and a menu; find ‘employees,’ and let’s go with it. The name, theme, and menu are up to you, and I will back you 100%, but the board will also need to give their thumbs up.”

“Thanks, Governor. I have pretty much decided on all of it. As for employees, several teens asked for a rotation in the mess, and a few of them are really good at it. So I want to make them the first employees.”

Marcus looked at his aide. “Put her on the board’s next agenda.” He walked to the line. As he did, he turned to her,

“Ev, an employee sounds like a job; job alludes to a paycheck. How will you provide pay?”

Since pay on Terra was not in credits but in trade. He understood. A day’s work for nothing. Marcus walked back to her, speaking softly, “How about we create a credit account? Work a while. Get a few points. The new barracks are finished. Your people can be the first permanent residents. There are 35 rooms available in the building, a few minutes from here. They are yours if you want them. Let your people know that once our visitors leave, they can move in. 4 are multibedroom apartments, so roommates?” He smiled at her, “Maybe management quarters?”

She grinned at him. He went to the line to get some food, and she headed to the back of the new restaurant. As she entered the kitchen, “DONE!” was all she said, and the staff cheered. You could hear it in the dining area. Marcus had to explain to everyone when he made it to the table. He had his tray and went to the others. The teams were grouped by profession at tables, and he saw the admin table had an opening. And since he was an admin, he sat. They asked about the cheering, and he let them in on the events.

As he sat, he noticed he had a steak. “Where did this come from?”

Izzy replied, “Well, Marcus, that is a devil cat steak, and our chef has been in your kitchen teaching your people the best way to prepare it. But, trust me, we know all the wrong ways to cook it.”

Marcus cut a small piece off and put it into his mouth. “This is great. Tastes like a cross between beef and lamb.”

“Yup, tasty!” Romeo said.

They planned for the next few weeks, Romeo heading to the lake, but instead of the ground transport and 5 hours of plush and beautiful desert scenery, they hopped in the shuttle. The pilots are on board with that plan, and Romeo has some ideas for the shuttle. The shuttle can really come in handy. He can bring a lot of house in that shuttle, then head back on the weekends later to hook it all up. An overnight campout is in order, maybe two nights if it takes longer than planned. Just Romeo and 3 visitors. Now, what can he prepare for dinner?

~~~~~~~~~~

“Looks like we got it all finished. The home link is solid. I guess you are better than carrying a forklift and a crane.”

“I guess. So how are you going to impress us with dinner?”

Romeo raised a finger to let them all know to hold their thought. Then, he pulled his small handheld radio off his belt and brought it to his face, “Wilomena, this is Romeo. The installation is complete, and this is the final test."

"I hear you. It's nice and clear, too. The best connection we ever had to the lake.” She replied over the radio. “You are on your HT? How far from the antenna?”

“Yes,” Romeo grinned, “I am on the HT, about 5 kilometers from the antenna, which is actually on the other side of the lake and at the top of Devil's Tower from my present location. The shuttle made it a fast install at the top, and maintenance should be minimal.”
~~~~~~~~~~

Wilomena's voice came back, "Excellent. We needed a repeater there, the highest point, and beautiful scenery. You can see our backyard mountain range from there." She paused, "OK, let me try a cross-connect. Marcus will call you through his desk comm, and you should get it where you are."

"OK, standing by," Romeo said.

A minute later, his HT beeped a few times. "Romeo here." He said as he pressed the button on the side of the Handheld Transceiver.

"WOW!" Marcus said, "I hear you perfectly. So now we can maintain a comm connection to the lake." Marcus got quiet momentarily, "Can this support data also?"

"Yes, why?" Romeo asked.

"Had a thought. We can monitor many things in that area, like filters, weather, etc. So maybe we can clear a few channels for that?"

"I like it. We can work on that after our guests leave."

"Thanks, Romeo. Have fun. You going to spend the night there?"

"We are, maybe a couple; got another little project I want to look at."

"I take it you are at your house," Marcus said. The others all looked curious.

"We are, but I guess I need to explain that to them." He paused, "OK, Marcus, thanks for helping with this test. Romeo out."

“One last thing. Can you verify the range of the HT to the repeater? Head north since that is how the hunting party heads when they head out.”

“Good idea. We will do that tomorrow. I have a few bikes, so we’ll let the shuttle crew relax in the living room. Wilbur and I can go for a ride.”

“Should be a nice day for a ride.”

“Yep. Maybe 3 or 4 hours north, and we can call the shuttle to get us instead of riding back. We’ll stop and test every fifteen minutes or so.”

“Excellent! Marcus out.”

He changed the channel and keyed up again. “This is Terra calling Rest Stop. I am testing the cross-connect of the repeater we set up and if the connection through the ARC is set correctly.”

A few seconds later, “Hi Romeo, this is Rachael. I’m holding down the fort here while Dad is with you.”

“Hang on a sec,” He handed the HT to Wilbur.

“Hi, Baby. How are things at home?”

“Hi, Dad. Does this mean all the comm is working now?” Romeo nodded.

“It does. If you need any of us, just call. You can get any of us on our personal radio. What is going on there? Anything I need to know about?”

“We lost a few more personal comm sets due to rust. If you can get more radios, that would be great.” She paused, “Oh, and let Izzy and the Major know that the rifles are starting to do the same thing. Evidently, the water here is more acidic than on Earth, so it was never tested in an environment like this."

"Call the Major yourself. You got the connection now. By the way, Romeo has a few crates of extra radios for us, and he is letting up borrowing a repeater."

Romeo yelled before Wilbur's finger let up on the talk button, "RENT! A repeater you can rent."

She laughed, "Tell him I'll pay the rent in those chocolate-chocolate chip cookies like I made at the training center."

"Deal," Romeo said.

"He agreed. Good idea. Anyway, I'll let you go. We are talking about food here, and Romeo is cooking."

"OK, Dad. Talk to you later. Rest Stop Comm out." Rachael disconnected and probably called the Colonel to tell her about the rifles.

He turned to the others, "Who's hungry?"

"Again, what's for dinner?"

"I thought about that before we left and came up with a great idea. When was the last time you had chili?"

"Well," Wilbur said, "It has been a while."

The pilot, Kevin Marsol, added, "Please tell me it has beans and veggies. Texas chili is so boring." The others all nodded in agreement.

“Well, gentlemen, you are in luck. This is my chili stew! It has taken first prize on two planets.” The others groaned when he joked, “I have some cornbread and a few additives for the chili, and yes, there’s enough for seconds for all of us.” Then, he winked, “If there are any leftovers, it goes well with eggs.”

“When do we eat.” All three of them said at the same time.

“Thankfully, I figured we would be doing this, so I cooked the chili and the cornbread the other day. All I need to do is reheat it, and we are good. I say maybe 20 minutes or so.” He pointed off to his left, “The sun is setting. Look off in that direction. It is pretty amazing in this desert. Look at the horizon, and let your mind wander. I see ghosts, birds, and dragons as the sun sets from here. This is my favorite place to be; before you ask, I create reasons to come out here.”

They all sat a moment in silence, in meditation or perhaps contemplation.

Romeo continued, “When we spread out from the colony, I plan to build a house. Already got it staked out.” He motioned to limbs, well-placed rocks, and large splinters of wood pounded into the dirt. They all saw the floor plan for his house, and as they ate dinner, he described the place in intricate detail. Room by room. It was a lot of fun, and the new friends offered ideas he incorporated into his future dwelling.

Wilbur asked about the backyard, and Romeo had already thought of it. The backyard was a place for family, friends, pets, and entertainment.

"Well, BBQ pit for me, the outdoor kitchen, of course. Handmade furniture and a jungle gym for the kids. Not just my kids but the entire neighborhood. Lots of grass to let the dogs play, three of them. Small, medium, and large."

Wilbur asked, "Names?"

Romeo grinned from ear to ear. He looked at them sitting around the fire, "The small one is Nina, the medium is Pinta, and the large one is Santa Maria. Santa for short."

The sun had already set, and the sky was completely black. However, the stars were shining bright. The fire they all sat around warmed them as the air cooled off. They dropped the wood on the fire and talked for a couple hours. After that, they needed to sleep; they could have all slept on the ship, which would have been more comfortable, but Romeo pulled out his bedroll and laid it a meter from the fire.

There was nothing too dangerous or deadly in this world, Wilbur joined him, but the pilots opted for the ship. "You guys can use the shower in the morning if you want. We got breakfast covered. See you in the morning." They headed to the shuttle and went in, leaving the door open. Nothing out here to do any damage anyway.

"Goodnight." Romeo and Wilbur said back to them.

"OK, and where are we sleeping?" Wilbur asked.

Romeo pulled out a couple huge trash bags, and they filled them with leaves and tree needles. Made for a comfy bed.

Romeo put a bit more wood on the fire so that it would burn smaller but for a longer time. Then, finally, he nestled into his sleeping bag, resting on a giant trash bag filled with leaves. Wilbur was in the same boat.

“You know, Romeo, this is pretty comfy,” Wilbur said. “How cold do you expect it to get tonight?

“It is. I like this. Maybe 8 or 10 degrees Celcius or so at the coldest. Not too bad, really.” He took a breath, “By the way, that sheet of plastic I gave you?”

“I wondered about that,” Wilbur queried.

“Spread it out and loosely lay it over you from head to toe. This may be a desert, but the morning dew will soak you like you fell in a lake. I learned this out here on day one. By morning, I felt like I had been caught in a rain shower. Been sleeping like this ever since, and with no issues. I hang them under the roof when I head back to the colony. I’ve come out here at times and seen them moved around.”

Wilbur laughed, “Is someone sleeping in your bed, Goldilocks?”

“Actually, yes. Anyone who needs to be out here uses my house as a base camp. Mainly because it is set up to be used as a base camp.” He snapped his fingers, “Remind me in the morning to leave a couple radios under the shelter so they stay dry.”

“I have a radio box you can have. We can mount it in the morning and put a few radios. It says EMERGENCY COMM in red on a bright yellow box, and it is airtight.”

“Perfect. After breakfast, we can do that before we head out on the motorcycles and test the range of the comm system."

They spread the plastic sheets over them and laid back on their makeshift mattress. In less than 2 minutes, they were both fast asleep.

~~~~~~~~~~~~

The smell of food cooking over an open fire woke the two campers. The pilots, Michael Roberts and Alexi Krovalov, had quite a sampling of foods already made. The steaks were just about done, and the coffee smelled heavenly.

"How long have you two been awake?" Romeo asked.

"Long enough," Alexi replied.

"Maybe an hour," Mike added.

Alexi said, "The chili was delicious, so I thought we could reward your effort. So, in a very vague sense, we have fresh coffee, scrambled eggs, hash browns, and a steak."

Romeo asked, "Vague.....sense? Please elaborate."

Mike replied, "Well, the eggs are powdered but taste good. The potatoes are a red tuber we found at Rest Stop. After grating them, we soak them in a nice brine for a day. It brings out their true flavor. Really close to an Earth potato and perfect for hash browns. You had one steak at the restaurant. Cat Steaks are cooked perfectly medium. As for the coffee...."

Alexi added, "...as for the coffee, it is real. We grew it on Rest Stop from seeds we carried, and I roasted the beans this morning over this fire. Then I hand-grounded the beans and made this pot of coffee for us. It should be enough for
~~~~~~~~~~~~

two mugs each. I have sugar and powdered milk you can add if you wish."

Romeo smiled, "The Rest Stop coffee company. Cannot wait to taste this. Is it different from our coffee?"

"Quite a bit different. The botanists say the heavier gravity makes for a deeper flavor profile. Since they are planted near a grove of what we call vanilla trees, they have a very slight vanilla flavor."

Romeo accepted Alexi's cup and took a black sip. "Damn! This is amazing. There it is, the vanilla aftertaste."

"Told you, we have much to offer each other," Will said.

"Can I get a bag of these seeds? Then, I may try growing them here and see what they become."

Alexi said, "I had that thought also." He pointed to a hillside near Romeo's future home, "I think right there would be the perfect spot to grow these little beans."

Romeo added, "Excellent. My house should be built in the next year, and we can give the Rest Stop coffee company its first franchise."

Will said, "Great, let's eat. I'm starved!"

CHAPTER SIX

Colonel Dryer and Marcus were meeting well before morning in her office.

"Got a call from Rest Stop last night. Our team at the lake connected everything and were having dinner. Wilbur spoke to his daughter, Rachael, and told me the rifles are experiencing a high failure rate due to acidic water, humidity, etc. She buzzed me and told me. So I am giving her a few more cases of rifles."

"Can we spare them?"

"Yes, not an issue. We can give every colonist on Terra three or four rifles for their own personal collection, so a few more cases will not be an issue."

"Approved. Do whatever you need to do. I trust you." Marcus said.

She was quiet for a bit too long, and Marcus looked at her, and finally, she spoke. "Marcus, we determined that Dayl Warrin is creating a group of dissidents, and his plans appear to be to leave the colony and start his own."

Marcus looked a little shocked, just a little. He seems to have known about this already. "Life here was not plush, but it was not that hard. So, Sarah, what do you recommend?"

She thought a moment, "How did you know about it?"

"I suspected. My son and the other Handies reported bits and pieces to me during our last couple of meetings. Dayl has been planning this for a while. The problem is that no one really understands the why of it all."

"Should I pull him in for questioning?" Sarah asked.

"No, let's see where this goes. None of the Handies think it will escalate to sabotage or violence. Instead, they feel the group will find a place and make a third settlement."

"So…. I say we let him leave. Give Dayl and his people what they need to get started and support if he runs into trouble."

Marcus was shocked. "You're serious?"

"I am. He has maybe 25 followers, all unhappy with their life, situation, or existence. If they venture out into the desert and create a town," she grinned, "Maybe a cult of some form, one of two things can happen. They will find their place in this existence or return to us with a renewed spirit."

Marcus thought a moment, "OK. Ask him to visit me. I will propose it to him." Then, pausing, "Where do you suggest they start their new home?"

"I thought about that last night. We can run a water line from the top of the collector to the west. Then, at least, they would have water. Give them seeds and some preserved food until their crops are harvested. They have enough time until winter to build homes or whatever."

Marcus sat there a minute, looking at the top of his desk. It was a hard pill to swallow; he felt like he had let this group down. Yet, somehow, he had no idea how they felt, and he took that all on himself.

"Let's go to breakfast and see our visitors." They stood and walked out the door.

"I'll meet you there. Something I need to do first." She turned and left.

Daylight was approaching. Soon, the new day would begin, and the town would come to life.

~~~~~~~~~~

Standing at the window, slowly dressing, she looked around her hotel room. Then, returning her gaze to the window, the outside world, she stopped. So different than home, she thought.

"Home!" she said out loud and smiled a bit.

Andrea Battle stood in her room in the barracks and stared out the window into the fading darkness as the sun was just beginning to rise. She slept well last night. The lighter gravity here on Terra is refreshing, but she knows she will pay for it when she returns home. Those trips to the Devil Cat planet can make your homecoming hell if you stay too long. But, going home, well, there is always a price to pay.

She had already walked into the hall, grabbed a cup of coffee, and returned to her room. They were thoughtful
~~~~~~~~~~

about leaving a robe in the room for use while on the planet. She sipped her coffee slowly as the view into the barely illuminated landscape put her into quiet and reminiscent contemplation. She remembered her first few days on their new planet after waking up on the ship after a long sleep. Learning about her new solar system and receiving her first trip to the surface, the first mission, to Rest Stop. She slowly dressed as she relived the first days out of stasis. She looked at herself in the mirror as she picked up her uniform. She liked what she saw and realized the body art covered most of her skin, but it was hidden entirely when she was in uniform.

She added the tattoos and ensured they were well hidden under her clothing. The art was for her, not for display. It commemorated an action, battle, or event in her life.

Yesterday, she heard of a tattoo artist in Cougarville. She hoped to get there today to speak to him. She had an idea for some new art, right between her breasts in the center of her chest. Kissing skulls.

Refocusing on her uniform, she stared at the pin on her collar. Then, out loud, not much above a whisper, she put her hand on the pin and repeated, "I.Y.A.A.Y.A.S." Looking out the window again, she let her mind wander. Her recurring daydream, a close friend of late, returned, and as she dressed, she relived good times. She relived day one after waking up from her long sleep.

“A little oasis in the big dark. We just happen to find this little rock out of sheer chance.” The Captin said at a briefing.

Nearly out of food on the ship, the ‘actual food’ rationing was about to force them to go back into stasis. However, they did not want to break into the emergency rations since those were preset for each person. Enough meal bars for each to eat one per day for about a month.

The 10 people awake were not ready for that when the computer announced a solar system a few days away with a planet matching Earth with a 79% viability. This means there was a 21% chance it would not support human life.

21%, better than the 100% chance of starving to death on the ship.

The Captain set the course and launched the Genesis probe. It would arrive a few days before them, and they would have a general idea of the planet’s conditions, at least 26 points on the surface.

As they entered the system, the ten awake made a choice after having one last feast. They would land and create a new life for themselves here.

The Science Officer, Rachael LeRoy, walked in, and after everyone was silent, “Well, we can survive on the surface. 29% oxygen, 67% nitrogen, the rest is random stuff, nothing bad. Plenty of vegetation, animal life, and it appears the veggies and critters, from what I can see from up here, are compatible with humans."

The Captain said, "That is great." Then, he smiled, "Sit and have something to eat."

Rachael stood there momentarily, the room quieted again, and she continued, "One more thing. Surface gravity is 52% more than Earth's standard. So if you weigh 100 kilos on Earth, you will weigh 152 on the surface here."

Someone commented, "That doesn't sound all that bad."

The Chief Medical Officer added, "Actually, that is bad. Less than 10% is not terrible and safe, but 52% will create a problem." She paused to collect her thoughts, "We will lose several people due to strokes and heart-related issues as their systems will not compensate for the added forces and the stress their bodies will be under. Those who survive will overcome the problem over time. For some, it may be several months before they can walk. But as I said, we will lose several of our numbers."

The tone of the feast changed. It became somber, and the doctor sat and had something to eat because she knew she needed to. Still, in the back of her mind, she wondered, as did everyone at the table, if landing on this planet would end their life.

They finished, cleaned up, and all went to sleep for the night as the ship orbited this new home for them. However, once 'morning' arrived and they all returned to the room, they decided to wake everyone up.

It took several days to wake everyone and a few days for all to be comfortable standing again. Then, they broke out the emergency rations. They have a few months of E-Rats on board and decided to let the probes accumulate more data before making a choice. The place where they would land the ship and begin their colony.

BEEEEEEEEP!

"Major Battle to the bridge." It came over the intercom system.

Droid shook her head as she stared out the window at the planet, her new home, for a moment longer. "Fuck this shit!" She spoke softly to herself, "We will survive. We need space, a place, a home to rest."

She abruptly turned into the passageway without making another sound, heading straight to the bridge.

The Captain did not give her a moment to breathe as she entered. "Major, we have onboard a small shuttle that can hold 6. You and your team will head to the planet below us for recon. We have the spot selected for you already."

She just looked at him, not saying a word. Finally, he got the idea and continued, “It appears as though it is a pretty safe location, and the environment supports our lifeform. We need a test. 2 pilots, 4 scientists, and 4 Marines.”

The Captain smiled at her, not a happy or fun smile, but the smile of someone dropping the other shoe.

“Droid,” He started again, “2 pilots, check. 6 seats in the back, check. 2 stow-aways sitting on the floor hoping not to become a steel ball in the pinball machine….. well, check also.”

She grinned at him, an evil grin for sure, but a grin meaning this sounded like fun. “That works. You 4 scientists for sure, but we only need 4 Marines. I would never sit in a seat if my Marines were on the floor, so the 4 Marines would be on the floor. That gives you 2 extra seats for more scientists for a 12-person team spending a week or two on the surface for recon and environmental verification.”

The Captain shook his head, “In that case, I’ll toss in a CMO and veterinarian. Perhaps you can find a few critters to verify.”

“Perfect.” She said. “By verifying, I assume you mean taste?”

The Captain laughed a little, “Thanks, I needed that.” He collected his thoughts, “Major, you are in command of this mission. Maintain radio contact, and be safe." He rested his hand on her shoulder, "Droid, find us a new home."

"Yes, sir." She rested her hand on his momentarily and gave him a friendly glance.

"One thing to remember, the gravity is half again more than Earth, so you may have issues. No, check that. You will have issues."

She looked at him. "So, walking with a 50-kilo pack on your back will feel like 75 kilos? Interesting." She turned to leave.

Walking out the door, she stopped in the passageway. She touched a panel and spoke, "Marines, gear up. Team 1, camping." She deactivated the comm and headed to the Marine area.

They stocked the shuttle for the next couple of weeks with food, water, and equipment, and the Marines packed what they needed separately.

The pilots would remain in and on the ship after landing, a control set of people. They would not live in the environment. Rachael Ross and Illiana Daskanova agreed to be the control subjects, eating and drinking only what they bring. Twice daily blood samples from everyone. They would run the blood samples and log them into the database. The data is accessible to all, including the ship.

They departed, and as they landed, they all had gravity issues. It was worse and more challenging than they had imagined. They spent a day sitting in their seats. No one even got up except to use the head. Once they could move at the end of the second day, the Marines went outside and walked around, more like stumbled around.

“Major Battle to Santa Maria.”

“Go ahead.”

“Gravity is worse than we imagined. It took us a day just to become mobile. One of the pilots, Illiana, is having a bad time with gravity. But the Marines are all mobile, and we are looking around. We are picking vegetables, fruits, flowers, and stuff to bring to the CMO to see if it will kill us. We should know more this time tomorrow.”

“Understood. Be safe.” The Captain disconnected the comm.

~~~~~~~~~~

“Droid’s personal log, day 15. We have been on the surface for two weeks, and it is getting easier to move around. Although I am getting tired and exhausted, I am just taking a dozen steps. 12 steps on a flat surface are like climbing a thousand-foot mountain. Illiana is no better. She is no worse either, so that’s good news. In this gravity, it really sux being a well-endowed
~~~~~~~~~~

female. Thanks, Mom. With the gravity, it feels like they are being pulled off. But I found the solution. Not a bra, but a boob girdle. I strapped the girls down a little tighter than usual, which seemed to help. The other females followed suit and agreed this was the way to go. Racheal laughed at us and commented that being a lifetime member of the IBTC may be suitable for this planet. At this point, having itty-bitty's proves to be less 'stress' on her, so yes, the less you have, the better." She laughed briefly.

"Oh, the gravity is also affecting the males. They created makeshift girdles for their man parts, I mean jock straps. Evidently, they were getting pain from the dangly things like the women were feeling. So, we need good tube tops and jock straps before landing."

She laughed, and her log recorded it, "For the record! That was the most ridiculous thing I have ever put into an official log." She laughed again, "Now, as for food and water. It rained pretty hard today for about an hour. We were all in our tents when the collected water was analyzed. We collected nearly 10 liters with all the sample spots we set up. The doctor said it is pure enough to drink as is, untreated. I tasted it, and although it is slightly floral, it is pretty good. We have been eating and drinking the local food and water since day 5. No side effects, and I recommend we stay a third week. I need to finish building my house anyway. As for food, vegetables are not bad. Strange look to what they taste, but I try every vegetable after the doctor OKs it. Both are in their raw and cooked state if she approves. Meat, well, we found these raccoon-size things that just walk up to us. They get into everything, curious little buggers. We are calling them HeyThere. As in, HeyThere, what are you doing? I am holding one in my lap now, and it is sleeping. Oh, and they purr. The vet gave one a thorough exam. They are vegetarian by nature and very tame. This tells me there may not be a predator on this world, so they have no fear."

"One was killed when we arrived, and the vet did an autopsy. Check his results for more information. It seems it was a mother, and the baby is an orphan now. The team is taking care of the little fur ball like a pet, which is really affectionate. One of the Marines, I will not say who decided to clean and cook it, and yes, we all felt a little bad about it, but after tasting it, we decided that it was not the best option as a food source. The meat is tough, has a very gamey taste, is stringy, and is extremely lean. However, we did find these little rat-sized things that have not been named yet but taste much better. Reminds me of a cross between beef and pork ribs. Maybe we can call them Borks." She laughed again, knowing the Captain would hear this shortly.

“Regarding food source, one of the vegetables contains nearly identical proteins as we have in beef. So, we can and will survive with sufficient amounts of this vegetable. I hope we have some creative cooks on the ship. This thing is REALLY bland. It is about the size of spaghetti squash and is bright red. It has a fairly thin skin and tastes a little like a cross between a turnip and a carrot, at least in its raw state. When boiled, it is more like roasted potatoes, but roasted in an oven, it takes on the flavor of Brussels sprouts. One serving a day is like the protein of a double hamburger. Mmmmm…. I may attempt to make a burger out of it and see how that goes. Never in my life did I consider eating a veggie burger.” She laughed again.

“Well, that’s my day 15 report. You should be getting this in a few seconds. Buzz me if you have any questions. I apologize for the commentary and the giggles, but this place is plain odd. You must see its humor, or it will make you nuts.”

Someone was pounding at the door and yanked Droid back to reality, “Hey, Kid, you awake. Let’s go grab some chow.”

CHAPTER SEVEN

Someone was pounding at the door, "Hey Kid, you awake. Let's go grab some chow." Gunny B, her birth mother, opened the door. "What are you doing? I need food!"

"Sure thing, Mom, let's grab something," Andrea replied.

Brendar the Barbarian stared at her and twisted her head slightly.

"What?" Droid asked.

"You were reminiscing, weren't you?" Mom asked.

"How did you know?"

"I remember when you were little. After some competition, debate, or test, you would grab a cup of tea, hot chocolate, coffee, or something and stare out the window, trying to figure out if you did everything you could; and no, it made no difference if you won or lost. It was about you living up to what you needed to be."

She smiled, "Guilty as charged." She hugged her Mom, "Let's get some food."

Brendar the Barbarian wore typical field attire. The current but 30-year-old version of fatigues or BDUs or field uniforms or whatever they are calling them now. The nameplate said **Brendar the Barbarian**. Andrea made it special for her before launch and gave it to her when they landed. She could not wear it at home; it was not official, but here, well, life is a little more relaxed. Her uniform fit her well and was designed to be comfortable in warm and cold weather. She always carried a matching coat in her pack, but it only needed a month or so out of each year.

Andrea wore a dark blue flight suit with the nameplate DROID in all caps. No rank. She had several patches on the sleeves identifying previous commands, missions, and the colony ship. Everyone had that patch, the Santa Maria, on their left shoulder. On her collar, she wore a pisspot. The universal symbol for AMMO. She was an ordinance officer for her first few years and enjoyed blowing things up. She was given the pin, highly polished silver, by the master gunny on the base. He was the top enlisted, and she learned a lot from him. He respected her because although she was, is, an officer, she listened before being 'in charge.'

They left the room and headed to the dining hall, “What were you thinking about?” Mom asked.

Tentatively, she spoke, “Well, Mommy, I remembered when we woke up. Those first few weeks, the fun on the planet and the chipmunk dinner.”

Gunny B said, “That was a fun camp. Alvin Stew is still my favorite recipe. We need to introduce it to these people here.” She took a breath, “Everything was so new and different. But the best part is that nothing tried to kill us!” She paused briefly, “Sorry that Bork never caught on.”

They laughed.

"By the way, you still wear that pisspot." Brenda said, "I bet you miss munitions?"

"I do. The people were amazing, a close-knit gang who would do anything for you."

"You still remember the motto?" Brenda grinned, "IYAAYAS!"

"Yes, Mommy, I remember." They recited it together.

"**I**f **Y**ou **A**in't **AMMO**, **Y**ou **A**in't **S**hit!" They howled, laughing as they left the room and headed to the mess.

Andrea said, "I need to order some of these pisspots. Maybe we can make it our logo or symbol or something."

"I like that!" Brenda replied. She was in the munitions field nearly two decades longer than Andrea, and their feelings about it are the same. The people, the friendships, the 'I got your back' attitude. This is what she missed about that job. This is what she needed to instill in her people. This is the future she had to have for those under her command. Work hard, play hard, loyalty, and friends; that's what it's all about.

"Mom, am I wrong that loyalty and camaraderie should lead people, and if they are in place, then everything else will also fall into place and…."

Mom said, "…and the world will be a better place, Huh?"

She grinned at her mom, "Actually, I was thinking of the universe, but the world is a good start."

They both laughed.

~~~~~~~~~~~

Gunny B and Droid sat in the dining hall alone. They had an excellent breakfast, and the coffee was amazing. It was peaceful, quiet, and….

Gunny K walked in, followed by half the people on this planet. Andrea and Brenda looked at each other and smiled, shaking their heads. "Serenity officially disrupted," Mom said.

"It was too quiet anyway," her daughter replied. They winked at each other.

Kathy walked up, "How long have you two been here?"

"Long enough. We had coffee, a great breakfast, and peace and quiet for a long time." Droid replied.

"What happened to the peace and quiet," Kathy asked.

Brenda said, "Not sure. But it was lost to the universe about a microsecond after you entered the room."

Kathy looked around, "Oh, I get it. They followed me in."

They all chuckled, "Let me grab something, and I'll be right back."

The Colonel walked up to the table and grabbed a seat, leaving three open at the six top. "Good morning, all." She said to the group.

"Colonel, did you sleep well?" Droid asked.

Marcus and Izzy filed out of the serving line and joined them at the table, followed by Kathy.
~~~~~~~~~~~

"Good. All present." Izzy remarked. "Marcus, you have the floor for the first half of this dispatch." Then, Izzy said, "I received a note from Earth last night, and I believe you received one also."

"I did," Marcus said, "I got a rather disturbing dispatch from Earth last night, and I need to pass it on to you." His face took on a serious tone, "It seems that Earth Command has seen fit to promote our Lieutenant Colonel to a one-star general, becoming the highest-ranking person in this or any other solar system outside of Earth. Furthermore, she is to assume command of all military in our colonies, Terra and Rest Stop."

Izzy did not look shocked but continued.

"My communique stated that a Major cannot be in command of the planetary forces." Andrea had an odd look on her face. "That is reserved for the rank of Lieutenant Colonel and above. Therefore, Major Battle is promoted to full Colonel in the Colony Protective Forces. Before you ask, yes, they changed the name of the military, and we are a branch of it here."

Both her parents stood and gave her a hug. Then hugged the new general.

Izzy said, "Now, that's not all of it." Everyone froze. "A Colonel needs subordinate officers, and all Gunnies are promoted to captain."

"WHAT?" they both said at the same time. "I can't be a captain. I'm enlisted!"

Droid smiled, “Not anymore.” The general stood next to her, “You are officers!”

“Yes, they are.” Then, the freshly minted general turned to the new Colonel, “Guess what? You can promote a couple to their old positions and find these two a job.”

“How about ordinance and combat officer for B, and Intel, training, and logistics for K?” Andrea replied, knowing full well EVERYONE was listening.

The general grinned, “How about for B, Ops Officer, and for K, Planning.”

“Hell,” Brenda said, “How about OPLAN and CONPLAN?”

Droid and Sarah looked at each other momentarily, then turned to the two former Gunnies.

“You know. How about we keep your former titles and call it a day?”

The moms looked relieved.

The General looked at them all, “I also discovered in the next year or so, after Earth’s light shuttles are put into service, command is sending us a few additional troops. They also asked how we can train them for life on Rest Stop due to the gravity.”

“So, I will need to determine how to not kill troops under my command from a planet with lighter gravity who want to experience and adapt to life on Rest Stop.”

The general nodded.

"Captains, you have a new job!" Although Droid and her commanding general just smiled, the captains shook their heads, simultaneously saying, "Yes, Ma'ams."

The message about the rifles at Rest Stop came up while eating, and the General said, "Captain Grimick will take care of it."

He just happened to be walking past the table, and the general stopped him and told him about it.

"Captain Grimick." The General said.

"Yes, general." He froze, "Captain?"

"Dispatch from Earth promotes all Gunnery Sergeants to the rank of Captain."

"Really? Cool!!"

Droid said, "Cool?"

"Yes, Ma'am. Very cool, actually."

The General continued, "Take our other new Captains to the armory and provide a few more cases of rifles. It seems the air on Rest Stop is detrimental to the mechanism's sensitive electronics and needs additional replacements."

"Got it covered, GENERAL."

He then snapped to attention and saluted her, and she threw a biscuit at him.

Someone at the following table spoke, "General, we have been working with a new waterproofing sealant for the buildings. It is easy to use, pliable when cured, and 100% air and watertight."

"Sadie, right? How is it on an active circuit?"

"Yes, general, Sadie Marcroft. We tested it at 1,500 volts and high current. That is as high as we can go at the moment. It is nonconductive at those levels. So, I would say it is pretty safe for the lower power of the internal electronics of the rifles."

"Can you and your group show this gaggle of captains the goup? I believe that is the technical term." The general was smiling at her.

"No problem. Maybe we can name it the General's Goup!"

Droid added, "How about Dryer Goup!"

Everyone said they loved that; that's the new name.

She and another at her table stood and walked off with the captains. Those at the table laughed, and the general gave a 'look' at each of them. She was kidding. It was pretty funny. Generally Speaking.

Everyone smiled at the turn of events. Then, settling into their seat, light conversation, food, and coffee. The morning started off perfectly. A short time later, the room cleared, and Sarah and Andrea sat with a cup of coffee.

"Droid, we have people in our little town who do not want to be here. So they will likely break off and start their own little town."

"What?" Andrea replied. "Let me guess. They are unhappy. They started stealing, calling it a redirection of assets, and are trying to gain more followers."

“OK, talk. I know what I am talking about. What are you referring to?”

“We have about 20 or so who are the same. They want to leave and start a place where they live by their rules, not ours.”

“Sounds familiar.” Sarah grinned, “I have an idea. Perhaps both groups would have a better chance if they joined forces and lived on this planet. We will run a water line to where they settle and give them seeds for growing food and comm units. Maybe you can do the same with your group. Fly them here, let them meet with our dissidents, and see if they are kindred spirits. If that doesn’t work out, the worst is you take them all home. But, if it works out, a third colony, a town actually, will be established on Terra, and everyone will win. I’ll let Marcus know. He feels like he let them down. But, he will feel better knowing that Rest Stop has a few like-minded folks.”

“I’ll pass this on to Izzy so she and Marcus can coordinate the plan.” She grinned, “I will suggest a video conference between the two groups as soon as we get home. They can bring any food, seeds, and fresh foods with them from home to help their new colony.”

They finished their coffee a while ago, but the conversation was enjoyable. They stood and headed to the door. Ready to begin a new day. Droid opened the door, “Please, general, after you.”

The general walked through, saying, “Thank you, Colonel.

They both smiled.

"What are your plans for today?" The General asked.

"I figured I would hike to Cougarville and do a little shopping. I hear a tattoo artist is there, and I have an idea."

"OH, you're talking about Rodney Westmore. He is amazing." She raised a sleeve and found a perfect image of the original Marine logo. I had a patch my great-grandfather received when he was a Marine. He put it on my arm. It is perfect. What are you thinking about?"

"I am mostly covered in ink, but my chest is bare. I was thinking about a couple of kissing skulls on my chest."

"Sounds like a plan. I get to see it when you are done."

"You'll be the first!"

"Have a good day. I need to take care of some security issues, our dissidents."

"Life is never dull in the colonies!"

The General looked at her friend, "NOPE!"

"The universe throws us curve balls, and we keep swinging," Droid replied.

CHAPTER EIGHT

Last year, the three colony ships were surprisingly reunited through transmission and a visit. Their brothers and sisters from Rest Stop arrived. They spent several weeks gathering the raw materials needed that were not present at Rest Stop, then returned home. They brought with them from Rest Stop a lot of preserved vegetables and proteins from their new homeworld in such an amount as to satisfy all residents of Terra and then some. In addition, the agro teams on Terra managed to retain an enormous amount of seed from their gift and hoped to grow new plants and strains from these unique seeds.

The conference call between Dayl's group on Terra and the group on Rest Stop, headed by Ramona Martin, went well. So well, Dayl and Ramona, close friends at the center before the launch, saw a spark in each other over the video. Everyone saw the spark these two had between them, and a few weeks later, a special transport made its way to Terra containing the making of half a new settlement.

Marcus and Dayl created the makings for the other half. They moved their group to the location the General and Dayl Warrin selected. He approved the site, expecting her to choose a bad area to start a new town. But she surprised him. The new place was beautiful, with enough wall panels to make about 30 buildings and houses. They would need to dig their sewage line, but that could wait. Latrines would work for now, and the construction equipment made fast work of it.

Each new structure had a built-in communications system, ensuring the group was not alienated from the colony. News feeds, local comm traffic, and videos from home. The Rest Stop group landed very close to the new town. They called it their spaceport and unloaded their ship, which also contained multiple buildings for use by the new town.

By winter, 65 single buildings were in the new town. Most were empty or used for storage since multiple people started pairing up. Regular runs between Rest Stop and Terra once a week made Tuesdays and Thursdays exciting for a time.

The new town was named Warrintown. The residents thought of honoring him for having the vision and creating a place where they could be who they wanted to be and not try to fit into some mold. This new town had many professions, including a few EMTs and Nurses. But, they would need to go into the colony for real medicine. At first, they tried to be 'apart.' But once someone was seriously injured, they knew they needed to head to the settlement for assistance.

Those in the colony did what needed to be done and had no judgment. Marcus saw to it that the people in the colony understood this new town was just that, a new town and not a place to look down upon.

When there was a party in the colony, they were invited, and when they showed up, they were treated like friends, not anti-social dissidents. Then, a new animal was discovered in Warrintown at the beginning of the following summer. This unique animal was tested, examined, and found to have a gland that secretes a chemical that boosts the immune system and kills bacteria. It is also somewhat effective against some of the local viruses. The animal, about the size of a small dog, is also the friendliest thing they have found, and as such, the households that have one as a pet are less sick than others.

They brought a few to the hospital and let them know the results of their basic test. After that, the hospital went more in-depth and learned this antibiotic gland is phenomenal. So, more tests are being run, and I hope the results appear promising.

Earth developed new light shuttles from the original plans and created small, medium, and large crafts. The first off the assembly line was the small, 4-person craft. Three of them were ready to depart and managed to get to Terra in under a month. This was the recon team scrutinizing the planet's area and everything between Earth and Terra. Two pilots, military types, and two scientists.

The trip to Terra was more of an accomplishment than a mission. They stayed a few days, then headed to Rest Stop. Unfortunately, at Rest Stop, one of the scientists developed a heart condition due to gravity. So they left two days after stocking the internal cargo areas with canned goods and the external cargo pods with fresh Devil Cat meat to bring back to Earth. They really need to come up with a new name for the meat.

The external pods were exposed to the vacuum and intense cold of space, so no refrigeration would be necessary. They tested it on the inaugural flight with various standard earth proteins. Nothing negative was detected.

Although all three craft were set up for external cold storage, one of the ships was partially set aside for packages to and from the colonies. This is where Marcus sent his friend the 18-kilogram gold rock for his desk. All wrapped up and addressed like a birthday gift.

Over the next year and a half, all three colonies grew, and personal craft began to appear. Romeo built his house near the lake and moved in alone. He planned for guests to have six bedrooms, each room with facilities. Large outdoor area and the most spectacular view anywhere on the planet.

He met a young woman, a nurse from Rest Stop. She had been there about six months and thought the gravity adjustment was complete when her heart decided to give way. A few weeks later, she was on Terra and, after a month, able to move around and work.

One afternoon, Romeo was repairing the communications array at the top of the cliff above the colony when a rock broke loose and rolled right over his leg. He called into the settlement, and Rebekka and a team of techs showed up in less than an hour.

She patched him up and cared for him until the cast was removed. They have been inseparable since. She adores the house and the fact they can be back in the colony in under 30 minutes with the new craft designed by Beeker. Romeo calls them a hover car, and Rebekka calls them all Grav-

Mobiles. They used an anti-gravity tech developed on Earth. They adapted for small applications like these cars, making it efficient to travel greater distances in a shorter time. Rebekka Martin and Romeo Rodriguez are on the same shift, so they commute from the lake home to the colony.

The repeater system was enhanced to be a full ARC; working from home is no different from the office. So, while he recuperated, he was never 'out of the office' except when he mysteriously disappeared from an available status for an hour or so. It seemed to coincide perfectly when Rebekka became unavailable. Coincidence?

Wilomena married one of the new security lieutenants, and they lived in her tiny house, where she had always been. The living room, kitchen, bedroom, office, and storage room are the size of a small bedroom. She loves the little house and has no intention of leaving it. Her husband, 1st Lieutenant Marshall Ricksbell, is the liaison to Earth and close to Marcus in that respect. Although, he technically does, and does not, work for Marcus. But why quibble?

Marshall was born in west-central Ohio and did his military training in Texas and California. Unfortunately, he had no family, so he volunteered for Colonial Security. Once he was accepted by Colonel Battle, he made his way to the spaceport in North Carolina, where he took his training and launched to head to the stars. His promotion to captain is due any day.

The general rule for all new security forces is an 18-month tour on Rest Stop if your body can tolerate it to gain muscle mass and density. Then, you can move on to your next assignment. That was established after Marshall arrived, so neither he nor Wilomena has ever been to Rest Stop. Frankly, neither has a strong desire to do so.

People from Earth visit Terra weekly for research, vacations, and a possible move to Terra. As a result, the colony has grown twice in population and nearly three times in layout.

Since the growth of both Rest Stop and Terra, Earth wanted to rename the position of Governor to President of the planet. Marcus and Izzy fought hard to let them know they did not like that and that Earth was their home base. So, they retained their titles as governors but were offered positions in the Senate. This meant more meetings; a few were on Earth, in person, and dull.

~~~~~~~~~~

Marcus sat in Owl Square on a bench his son had made just after they had arrived. He loved it here. It was peaceful, quiet, and serene. The colony communications unit, attached to his belt, chirped and vibrated. Marcus plucked it off his belt and brought it to his mouth, “Marcus here.”

“Sir, can you please come to orbital control? We have guests on arrival approach.” The young woman said.

“Guests? We are not expecting anyone. Are they coming in from Rest Stop or Earth?” He asked.

“That’s just it, sir. Neither. Somewhere in between and about 45 degrees above.”

Marcus’ face grew concerned, and he replied, “See you in ten minutes.”
~~~~~~~~~~

"Affirmative, sir. At their present speed, they should arrive in about an hour."

"Alert the general. Marcus out."

He headed to the spaceport and arrived moments before the general. "Well?" She said.

"Well, what? You know as much as I do." He smiled at her, and she gave a slight nod in return. Together, they entered the building and approached the woman who called them.

"REPORT," the general said.

"Not much more than I already told you. The craft appears to be a space vessel three times as long as wide, and this thing is pretty long. It is powered by ion propulsion, and wait…." She stared at a screen, "The ion drive cut off, and it's slowing." She checked a few readouts, "Yep, they are transitioning to a type of gravity drive, and it looks as though they are preparing to make orbit and land."

The general tapped a console. "LAUNCH. DEFEND. But for god's sake, do not start a fight." She looked at the console operator, "ETA?"

"…less than two hours till orbital insertion. Security flights 1 and 2 launching." The six small and fast crafts headed up. As the two fighter craft headed to rendezvous with the alien craft, Marcus called Izzy.

"Izzy, code 7," Marcus said.

"Understood. Standing by." She replied, and the connection terminated.

Isabella tapped a console, "Colonel. Terra just called code 7. You have launch clearance at your convenience."

"Understood, Governor." Colonel Droid stated, "Launching in 5 minutes with an ETA at Terra in under one hour."

Droid called it by the numbers. "FUEL!"

"FUEL, Check."

"PREHEAT!"

"Preheat underway. 79 seconds remaining."

"WEPS!"

"Weapons prepped. Plasma cannons are good, as are torpedos, full load, tubes loaded, and arming set to one kilometer."

"PERSONNEL!"

"All personnel are onboard. Captain Gunny's ETA on the bridge is 15 seconds. Doors closed and sealed, ship pressurized and stable."

From off to one side. "Colonel, we are cleared and ready for launch."

Without a second thought, Andrea Battle, Colonel Droid, yelled, "LAUNCH! Once in the upper atmosphere, kick in the big engines and don't spare the horses. 100% is the minimum."

"Bridge, engine room."

Gunny B responded, "Engine room, bridge, go."

"Captain, we are currently ascending at 114% nominal velocity. Space in 8 seconds. Engines are ready to jump with 134% efficiency, giving us a 49-minute transition to Terra."

"Understood." Captain Brenda Battle replied. She hated being called Captain, so everyone still calls her Gunny B.

Droid looked at her Mom, "Kiddo, we got it covered. Just hope we get there in time to help."

"You and me both, Mom." Andrea glanced at the empty seat next to her.

Gunny B said, "She'll be fine. She's on cleanup."

Droid smiled and nodded. The second ship, launching 30 minutes after the first, is a backup surprise reserved after the first ship arrives. This attack craft is heavily armed with a new breed of weaponry and strategy to finish the battle and the war if necessary. Today is their first activation.

Gunny B opened the comm, "Gunny Marsh to the bridge."

A minute later, a very tall and muscular man entered the bridge. He took his seat next to Brenda and reported.

"Colonel, OPS manned. Receiving telemetry from Terra." There was a slight pause as he reviewed the data. "Ship appears to be a kilometer long and ion propulsion. Currently transitioned to gravity drive, slotted to enter orbit, and land at Terra SpacePort. ETA is 90 minutes. Our current ETA and speed are 37 minutes to the system plus 6 to orbit. So we will be in orbit before them. Ship 2 will be 35 minutes behind us."

Droid said, “Governor, general, did you get that?”

“We did. Good timing.” General Dryer said.

No one spoke. They watched the screen, consoles, and each other.

“Entering system, orbit in 4:30.” A pause, “4 minutes to orbit.”

“General, anything new?” Gunny B asked.

“Nothing. Alien craft holding short of orbital insertion.”

Gunny B asked. “Colonel, permission to press the pedal to the metal?”

She nodded, and the ship lurched forward.

“Firing forward thrusters…..” a pause, “Orbit achieved. Stationary nose to nose with unknown craft at 100 kilometers.”

The general asked, “OK, Droid. Now what?”

Droid glanced at the comm tech. “Sergeant McMichaels. Open all channels.”

“Open.”

On the bridge, the sir and ma’am were dropped for efficiency.

“This is Colonel Andrea Battle aboard the attack craft Scorpion. Please identify yourself and your intention.”

30 seconds later, “Dees eez Marzo of dee Alliance. We meen yuu no harm. Wee arr here to say hello and,” She spoke to someone in a language they did not understand,

"Apologeez, Wee are here to say hello and welcome you to the area and to introduce us to you."

"You speak our language?" Droid asked.

"Not really. We recently heard your transmissions. I believe you call it the blue channel. Fascinating communications systems. We understand the principles and have developed something similar in our worlds. As we saw in many of your transmissions, you seem like humans who will not shoot first and ask questions later."

Droid laughed, "Marzo, can I assume this is a friendly visit, not an invasion?"

"Yes, Colonel, we are here to represent our many species and our alliance."

"Alliance?"

"Yes, 31 worlds all helping each other. Supplies, personnel, technology, and I believe you call it a vacation."

"Your language skills with English are improving geometrically."

"We understand language. I am the leader. This is the Exploration craft…." Marzo thought again, "I have no idea what the word in your language would be.

Droid asked, "Can you describe it to me?"

"Our hill country has an open place, a large green expanse. We go to places like this to concentrate on our mental and emotional well-being."

Droid smiled, "I know the place, an open field where you can be at peace and one with nature. I call it Serenity."

"YES!" She cackled, "Serenity, a serene place. Quiet, peaceful, and friendly."

"Standby a moment, Marzo; Colonel Battle to all ships and command centers; stand down. The Alliance craft Serenity is here to greet us as friends."

Marcus spoke, "Marzo, this is Marcus, the governor of Terra. Can you land on the planet so we can meet in person?"

"We can. We have a smaller craft, which is similar to your cargo shuttle. It contains gifts for you from the Alliance."

"Do you breathe oxygen?" Gunny B asked. She sent the image of an oxygen molecule, hoping they would understand.

"Yes, we call it razz, and we can easily survive in concentrations greater than 30% of the atmosphere.

Droid muted the comm, "B, open private comm with Gunny K. Instruct the Wasp to remain in orbit and perform a full scan of that ship. Once complete, at her discretion, land or remain in space. Assign the Terra attack craft at her discretion."

B nodded and took care of it.

"Serenity, please follow us to the landing area," Droid said. "Be advised the razz level on this world is a bit lower than you may be accustomed to, so take precautions as you need."

"Thank you." A small craft, the same or similar size to the Scorpion, left from the Serenity. "Scorpion, this is Serenity Shuttle following you."

"Best speed to the spaceport." She looked around, "Marcus, put out the good china. We have guests for dinner."

CHAPTER NINE

Both ships landed at the spaceport nose to nose. The Colonel asked why the ship landed that way. The pilot, Lieutenant Alex Raymond, replied, "No real reason other than it looks cool."

B shrugged her shoulders and said, "OK then."

"Shut it down. Open the doors. Let's go introduce ourselves to our, hopefully, new friends." She looked around, "Mom, Alex, Draya, you're all with me. Mom and Alex, side arms only. Drays, standard."

They all left the bridge and warmed up. Only Draya Ashani needed to get a weapon, the rifle. As she approached the ramp to disembark the ship, she reached and pulled a rifle from its place in the wall without slowing down. All members wore sidearms at all times. It was a part of the uniform. The ramp finished opening and touched the ground. As the ramp touched, it made a small dust cloud. By the time it did, they were already almost down. They stepped off the ramp as the puff of dust settled, and when the ramp hit the surface, the group walked to the other ship.

No sound, but the wind was blowing in from the hills to the left. Andrea approached the airlock and, jokingly, knocked after a few moments. Their door opened.

Several aliens strolled out of the ship. They looked human-ish primarily, with a few differences. The color was mainly black, but a couple had huge black eyes, and others had small eyes with a bluish tint to their skin. One woman looked like an animal of some type, perhaps a coyote.

Andrea approached the group, “I am Colonel Andrea Battle. We spoke in space. I took it at your word; this was a peace delegation.” She glanced down at the weapons worn by each member of the party.

“Ah, yes. You do not understand yet. These are ceremonial weapons from our history. They are worn only in such instances or at planetary meetings, which I dislike.”

“So, you cannot harm others with them?” She asked.

“Well, if I remove it and hit you with it, it will hurt!” Andrea and her team started laughing. When the general and the others from Terra saw, they approached.

Andrea spoke loudly, “Secure all weapons. Gunny B, get my swords.” Brenda ran to the Scorpion.

They spoke at the shuttle for a few minutes as Captain Brenda Battle brought her daughter a set of swords given to her when she was commissioned. She removed her pistol and handed it to a soldier with the Terra group. He slung it over his shoulder, and she strapped on the sword.

“There, this is our ceremonial weapon. A sword forged on our home planet several lightyears away, presented to me by my mother when I was commissioned into military service.”

“Your mother presented this to you? It is a fine weapon, quite beautiful and elegant in design. We have nothing similar in any alliance world.” She paused, “I would like to speak to your mother regarding this… this….”

“We call it a sword.” Brenda Battle replied. “And you can speak to me about it. I am Colonel Battles' mother.”

“You?” she appeared shocked.

“Yes, ma’am. Although I am her mother, I have been in service to my world for nearly twice as long as my daughter.

Brenda handed the other sword, a matched set, to Andrea.

“Marzo. I wish to gift you a matched sword in the truest form of peace. These two were created as a matched set, and one day, my mother told me when I found the right person, I could give this sword to them as a symbol of friendship, peace, and unity.”

Marzo accepted it with joy.

Both identical swords' blades are 44 centimeters long and made of highly polished titanium. The sword has a razor edge, making a scalpel appear dull by comparison. The scabbard is gold-plated titanium, lustrous, with an ornate design etched into the gold. The hilt and handle are solid gold plated surgical steel with silver inlay, ‘A. BATTLE.’

“Marzo, this is my name,” She pointed to A. BATTLE on the plate. “These two swords are duplicates of each other, hand-made by a craftsman nearly 100 years ago on my homeworld. They were updated and cleaned; my name was added to both almost 45 years ago. My mother always said one day, I would know to whom the second sword was destined to be given. Today is that day." Everyone looked at Brenda. She had tears in her eyes.

Marzo removed her weapon and handed it to someone behind her. Andrea needed to instruct her how to fasten it, but once it was on, it looked good.

All others attending the proceeding remained very silent for the past few minutes, realizing the intense ceremony this took on for the colony. Then, finally, Marcus spoke, "Marzo. I am Marcus, the governor and the leader of this colony. It is my pleasure to welcome you to Terra."

"Thank you, Marcus. My full name is Marzo Nuteq. I am the leader of the Alliance of Planets, and we thank you for your hospitality."

Andrea looked a little shocked, "Wait, I thought you were the leader of that ship. So you are the leader of the Alliance?"

"I am. I assumed you understood that Marzo was my title; Nuteq is my name. As the current Marzo, I am responsible for visiting new worlds and discovering those we consider to be in line with our minds. I believe you call it 'light on the trigger.' A shoot first and ask questions next attitude is never optimal in a primary contact event."

Marcus spoke. "On our world, your equivalent would be the Earth President. Ruler of our planet, the colony worlds including Terra, where we are standing now. Our president completely agrees with preserving life."

Marzo Nuteq smiled, "This sounds like the beginning of a friendship and an alliance." Then, she paused, "I would enjoy discussing with your President."

Andrea spoke, "Marzo, our home world, Earth, is four lightyears from us. So, your ship, how long would it take for you to travel the distance light would take in four years?"

From behind her, "Marzo. Using the human equation, I calculate if the speed of light is 300,000 kilometers per second." Andrea nodded at the new speaker and understood that her calculation was correct, "In that case, the transition to Earth would take a bit more than one revolution of this world."

Andrea added, "We measure time in seconds, minutes, hours, and days. One revolution of the planet is one day. It takes 22 hours on this planet. One second, well," She thought for a second, and then it hit her. She snapped her fingers and said, "These snaps are about one second apart."

The new person spoke, "Thank you, Colonel, that is extremely helpful."

Tonya spoke, "Marzo. We have three meals per day. In the morning, we eat breakfast. At midday, we have lunch, and in the evenings, we have dinner. You arrived just before our lunch, and we would be honored if you and your party would have a meal with us."

"Interesting?" Marzo Nuteq said, "Most people would invite me to the meal, leaving the rest of my party out of the invitation."

“Not here. We have another saying, the more, the merrier. If we got to know you, that would be fine. But getting to know your entire party would be amazing. I see different species, genders, and colors. It is an opportunity we cannot pass up.”

“I see two colors of people here.” The lead protector for Serenity said, “Black and white. Is your world black and white?”

“Actually…” Tonya paused, waiting for the introduction.

Marzo added, “This is Topen. She is, I believe, our equivalent of your Colonel.”

Tonya looked at Topen, “So I assume she has someone over her? We have the General over the Colonel. As for the colors of humanity, no, Ma’am. Although the predominant colors are black and white, there are red, yellow, and brown. We have two genders, male and female, but for some people, that is not a clear definition.”

“I do not understand?” Topen looked at the sky and said, “We have two genders. Male and female. Deemed by the location of their reproductive organs. Female is internal, and male is external.”

Tonya and most women laughed a little, “Similar here also.”

Marzo asked, “I would like to learn more about your physiology.”

Marcus said, “Let’s do that after lunch. I am hungry, and the restaurant is preparing meatloaf today. My favorite.” He got serious and asked, “You eat meat, right?”

"If by meat you mean the flesh of lower animals, then yes. Most of us enjoy it also." Her party laughed. "A few do not."

"We have some who do not also; we call them vegetarians, meaning they have a plant-based diet. So we have a large menu all will enjoy."

"It seems you are tolerant of a great many differences in your population?"

"We are, in a way. We feel that differences, diversity, and uniqueness add to our ability to adapt, overcome, and survive. We have made this new and different world our home through our differences."

"That Governor has a very healthy attitude." She smiled, which looked odd, and made Marcus return the smile without even trying.

"Then please follow me to the dining facility."

The procession led by Marcus to the dining hall walked through the town, and he managed to give a tour and some history of their place in the universe. Andrea added bits and pieces of Rest Stop as she saw fit.

A few of Marzo's party are from higher gravity planets and would also like to visit there.

Marzo Nuteq said as they approached the dining hall, "Colonel, perhaps you and a few of my party can visit Rest Stop for a few days. You can take my shuttle vehicle. It can get there in a few minutes. Although I am impressed with the speed of your shuttles."

Andrea cut her off politely, “Marzo. Colonel is my title. We are a bit informal here, and I prefer my name, Andrea, or my nickname, Droid.”

Marzo stopped and stared at her, “The word Andrea, in my home language, is…. Shall we say impolite?” Marzo shifted on her feet a little, “Let’s see, as plain and delicately as I can put it.”

“Marzo, please, just say it,” Andrea said. The rest of her party looked shocked, as she had said, Andrea.

She leaned close to Andrea and whispered, “In my native language, it is a derogatory word for where you go for organic waste facilities.

Brenda looked at the two whisperings; without warning, Andrea laughed.

“OK, What’s up,” Brenda asked.

Andrea looked at Marzo, “Leave it to my mother to give me a name like that.”

She leaned over to Brenda and whispered, “Mom, my name means toilet in her language.” Brenda started laughing, too.

“I hope I have not offended?” Marzo said.

“No, Ma’am.” Brenda and Andrea said simultaneously.

Andrea walked close to Marzo, “Is Droid good?”

Marzo smiled and said, “That means to honor in my native tongue.”

“Marzo Nuteq,” Droid extended her hand, “Allow me to introduce myself. I am Colonel Droid of the Earth and Colonial Protective Forces.

Marzo and Droid shook hands, “A pleasure to meet you, Colonel Droid.”

Marzo’s entire team started to relax and smile a bit.

The ice has been officially broken.

CHAPTER TEN

Earth has been a member of the Alliance for more than a year, and Terra and Rest Stop are destinations for Alliance member worlds. However, it seems that the gravity of Rest Stop is low compared to a few of the other members, who feel Rest Stop is a vacation destination. Therefore, they have a treatment that temporarily allows your body to function in a heavy-gravity environment. However, you still tire easily and need to rest a bit more. But, the outcome of heart and health conditions is averted.

The language barrier has been broken, and most humans can now speak Alliance standard. It is impressive that the Alliance does all it does and does not ask for anything in return. There is one exception.

The only rule is to hurt no lifeform. Marcus calls it the nice tax, and he does so in jest. Although life forms refer to sentient life, they use animals for food in some worlds, and Earth and a couple others keep them as pets also. Others, not so much. But all in all, some fruits and vegetables provide proteins and minerals.

One planet, in particular, is an entire planet of vegetarians. They are not vegetarians out of choice but have no native consumable animals. The rodents on the planet are deadly to them if consumed. A protein in the meat seems incompatible with the planet's primary lifeforms.

Since the Alliance has been around, the Colonies have been better off. They also rapidly assisted in the cleanup and rehabilitation of Earth, bringing it back to its pre-1700s condition in less than two years. As a result, the planet is beautiful, clean, safe, and abundant.

Colonel Droid has become a force. She and her teams have flown to many planets to demonstrate Earth's weapons technology and strategy. But, unfortunately, she was introduced to a plague of sorts. They are on the edge of Alliance space and have encroached and decimated ships as they pass close by to their attack lanes.

Droid took an Alliance ship filled with her Marines from Rest Stop and flew close to where the attacks occurred. She got her wish, and the marauders emerged from a nebula and made a beeline for the cruise ship. They docked and boarded the ship, not realizing that 40 highly trained human marines were waiting for this exact moment in time and space. They made fast work of the unwitting boarding party and headed into the ship, putting down every marauder they came to. Once the ship was theirs, they downloaded its database and wiped all data. Found the direction to their homeworld and sealed the corpses in, putting them on a destination for home.

Droid returned the data to the Alliance, hoping something like their name could be discovered. Why they were doing this would also be good to know.

After a few months, Marzo Nuteq called for the Colonel to visit her office on the Alliance home planet. She was given a debriefing regarding the data she returned. Captain B, Captain K, Isabella Zee, Marcus Samuel, and the General, Sarah Dryer, attended that meeting. The last few hours of the meeting were a strategy session to see what they could do about this threat to the Alliance and its citizens.

Gunny B is well known on several of the Alliance worlds also, but for her ability to use a variety of weapons and also her explosives knowledge. The Alliance had nothing like det-cord; she just happened to bring some with her. She casually removed it from her backpack when she saw someone removing trees in an area and asked if she could assist. She wrapped the cord around the four trees that needed removal and set a cap. Then, walking several meters away, she pressed a button on a controller, "Fire in the hole!" she yelled as the det-cord exploded. The trees were cleanly sheared off at the exact level they needed to be cut. The trees all jumped to one side and landed on the ground.

A moment later, they fell over exactly where they needed to fall so the crews could cut them into smaller sizes and remove the debris. For no other reason than this, she is a hero to the people of the Alliance. The event video was broadcast to all worlds and made its way back to Terra, Rest Stop, and Earth.

Earth is a destination location for the Alliance since it is so new. They do not need to limit visitors since the Alliance helped rejuvenate the planet. It appears Earth is an anomaly, 2/3 covered in water. Desalination technology is universal, and Earth found many water-ice snowballs in the asteroid belt that can be used on many planets. Several Moons in the Earth system are water-rich, and removing water from a frozen world has little to no impact on the planet or moon. The earth helped the Alliance from day one, and the Alliance is proud of the new member.

Beeker worked at an Alliance facility for a time and learned a great deal. Then, with his creative mind, he adapted one of their engines to his favorite shuttle. The result was speed greater than imagined and faster than any current Alliance exploration ship. He still lives at Rest Stop but consults and travels as needed. The Alliance shipyards seem to be in high gravity, and he adapts rapidly. The advantage is that ships built on the surface of a high-gravity planet can take more pounding.

They asked him to come on full-time in the development group, a multi-world section specializing in improving all types of transportation. After learning this new engine type, Roger has done quite a bit, becoming their golden child. In addition, it seems he has considered creative ways to adapt the engine that no other engineer has considered.

He asked if he could bring a few hovercars to the two planets, and they sent him a ship containing 50 small personal vehicles. He put 15 on Rest Stop and the rest on Terra. They allowed the colony to expand more than if they were on foot or horseback, so it was a win for everyone.

~~~~~~~~~~~

Before they left Earth space on their journey more than three decades ago, each colony member spent several years training. Military training for life in the Colonial Forces is a
~~~~~~~~~~~

multi-year education. Life will be challenging, and the training will hopefully make it easier. The development of the training center in central North Carolina has expanded several times since its creation. The Youngsville Complex was the first, with the survival center in Boone built next and the Ashville Technological facility third.

Youngsville, North Carolina, was the first stop for everyone destined to be a colonist. Basic skills training and farm education, primarily. Then, a person went to Boone to hone their outdoor skills and finally to the Ashville campus to become familiar with the technology used by CF.

The Youngsville Training Facility, located in the northwest section of the town, is bordered by three roads. Northbrook to the west, Bert Winton to the north, and Flemming to the east. To the south are a variety of businesses and housing developments. The fenceline for the facility is roughly two miles. The southern edge of the training facility has a small stream to educate the students in water reclamation, processing, and diversion.

The campus has six buildings, the largest of which is the residence. Single rooms for each student with a few multi-room apartments used to house and train families. Children are taught their current education level, but some basic classes include survival, farming, and security training. Weapons training for all over the age of 10 is mandatory.

The facility was initially built in 2041, the second to the last 4-year term of office for the Mayor. The residence hall was renamed FONZIE HALL when he decided he would not run again as mayor. He had no aspirations of seeking a higher government office.

Fonzie Flowers was mayor for nearly 30 years and witnessed many changes in his small rural town for the better and the worse. When he took over as town leader, it was small. Today, it is the hub for the colonial force's training facility.

Yes, there are a lot of other facilities around the globe teaching various courses to students. Still, every student must spend at least 13 months at this facility to learn the basics. Survival skills and weapons are a recurring theme.

Participants are dropped into the wilderness for the final exam, given a map and compass, and nothing else except for what they packed in their daypack. These are the 15 essentials of survival. In addition, each person can carry two meal bars, but you are given points if they are uneaten when you complete the course.

High-altitude drones watch out for the safety and security of each group of three or each family unit. Hopefully, the participants are unaware of this fact. The hike typically takes between 14 and 30 days, depending on the training course level the student is enrolled in. This is to weed out someone who cannot overcome hardship and even enjoy the oddness of the situation.

They were taught the art of camping by trained survival experts. For several months during the winter, they made camp in the woods on the campus before heading to the other facilities to enhance their education. Even the instructors stayed in the shelters they built to not diminish the need to have this skill under your belt. These skills gave the colonists the tools they needed to survive on arrival. Arrival on both Terra and on Rest Stop.

With most of the instructors now in their mid-70s, it is safe to say that camping in the wild may not be in the plan.

~~~~~~~~~~~

"The contingent from Earth is due today, and they said they have a nice surprise for us," Marcus said to Izzy over the comm system. They were in full video mode.

"That sounds ominous. What time are they due in?" Izzy asked.

"About 1600 local time, so maybe 7 hours from now. You gonna be here by then?"

"Yes!" She laughed.

Pausing a moment, Izzy muted and asked a question to someone off camera.

"Sorry, I asked for a special flight to visit you. I always wanted to fly on a fighter ship. Well, I get my wish. See you at 1330."

"That actually sounds like fun. Take pictures and give me a book report."

"I plan to if I am not too freaked out. Three seats, hyper capable."

"Yes, three seats in a ship the size of a closet with the power of a starship. I love our new friends; they have taught us a lot and helped Earth recover, but the tech they gave us is creepy." Marcus said.
~~~~~~~~~~~

"You mean a star drive engine the size of a watermelon? No, seriously, what is so freaky about that?" They both laughed.

"3 seats, so you, the pilot, and who else?"

"Well, me for sure, sitting in the mezzanine. I guess the colonel is coming, but I have no clue if there is a third, and she is flying, or the third is the pilot." She muted again, "Well, that's particularly interesting. The colonel and I are passengers, and the pilot is on his first solo with passengers."

Marcus cracked up at the look at her face, "Good luck!"

She changed the subject, "Anyway, who is arriving today?"

"All I know is they have a surprise for us, but they let slip that the gang from the training facility is coming to visit. They are like forty years older or something but interested in what we have done in the past decade on Terra and Rest Stop."

"Training facility? You mean the Youngsville Training Complex. The people who taught us about camping, wilderness, basic survival, water cleaning, and…."

"…yes, Izzy, and pooping in the woods. It ain't pretty, but it was necessary. There are a dozen of them making the trip. They hope to create a new program for future colonists, version two. Youngsville was maybe an hour from where we resided during phase two training, but they showed us a great time there. I hope they bring us some delicacies from the town center."

"Let's see, if I remember correctly, you were a regular at Scoops." She said.

"Yes, Scoops on Main Street! I popped in every chance I got after I had a nice deli sub next door. What was the name of that place?"

"Charon's Deli. And do not ask how I know that." She laughed. They both knew the names of both. It was within walking distance from the facility, near the train tracks. Maybe 3 kilometers from the facility, but using the railroad walking trail created after the trains stopped running through the town was beautiful.

By the later years of the 21st century, the use of trains to move goods was eliminated thanks to sub-orbital cargo craft. An adjacent community, South Hill, Virginia, became the cargo hub for the central/southeast United States. In addition, most of the rail lines were converted into walking or hiking trails. These trails spanned the entire country, and most countries followed suit by the end of the century.

Through the vision of the town leadership, Youngsville saw the writing on the wall. Terraforming, commerce, and goods distribution brought people from major cities into the area, and smaller towns grew; homes appeared. Along with an increased population, the town leaders expanded and developed the roadways, infrastructure, and shopping areas locally to match or exceed the ever-expanding population. Although rare, traffic jams did occur and were typically through incidents or accidents.

Overall, Youngsville became a model township – a case study for the rest of the world – on how to keep up with keeping up.

The first structures built in the compound were the barracks and the training facility. It was a serious boom to the central North Carolina economy since nearly all construction workers and contractors were employed for years to get this facility developed and built as quickly as possible. The barracks can comfortably house over 1,000 residents on the six floors above the dining facility. The 7-story building has a unique design. It was a square with about a ¼ kilometer on each side. The center of the structure was open and primitive land where camping and training could take place safer than in the actual wilderness – at least at the beginning of the training. Residents could walk in the grass, plant a small garden, tend to flowers, or sit under the shade of a tree and read a book.

A packed dirt path 10 meters from the outside wall of the barracks goes entirely around the entire residence building for anyone to use. One complete spin around the track is 1 kilometer from start to finish. Physical training is a large part of the requirement to be a future terraformer or colonist; everyone must partake in physical conditioning, regardless of age.

Each side and each floor of the structure has roughly 30 rooms, with singles on the upper floors and two or three-bedroom apartments on the lower. The multiple-room flats were reserved for families.

The training center was a few minutes away to the west, a beautiful walk across the campus. It was a two-story building, more or less, but had close to the same footprint as the residence area. The training center contained about 75 classrooms ranging in size from small, holding maybe a dozen people, to being able to fit an entire house, used to instruct on colony creation once you land at your destination. Construction classrooms, lecture rooms, briefing rooms, and study rooms made it the best training center on the planet.

CHAPTER ELEVEN

"Terra control, this is Shuttle Magma. We are leaving the main ship in a geosynchronous orbit. ETA to wheels down is 8 minutes."

"Magma, Terra control. You are cleared to land at your convenience. Parking at spot one, of course. Look for the flashy blue lights if you get lost."

The others in the room looked at her, wondering why she said what she did. "Terra Control, thanks. I'll pull over and ask for direction if I have a problem finding those flashy things." There was a brief pause, "But I brought you a nice bottle of cognac that I know you will share with my co-pilot and me."

Shiela smiled. She had been asleep for three decades. But life continued back to Earth. Her cousin Monica, essentially the same age as her, is the shuttle pilot. Monica's co-pilot is her husband, Lamar. Since Terra came online, they have been in the program. They looked forward to piloting the ship to visit Terra for almost a decade. So, when they heard from Shiela over the ARC, they knew they needed to be on the team to travel there one day. Now that the solar drive is in use, it is not all that long of a trek to Terra from Earth.

Shiela married just before the launch, and her husband is in the security forces. Digital security. He monitors systems. He works for Romeo and Wilomena, but they leave him alone to do what he needs to do. There is not much need for a systems security manager, but they still need someone diligent.

A few minutes later, the shuttle landed, shut down, cooled a bit, and the hatchway opened. First were the dignitaries and the instructors, the replacement crews, and finally, the shuttle crew.

As they shut down, she looked at her boss with a look – unmistakable. “GO!” he said. She jumped up and went to the shuttle to visit her cousin, their first-ever in-person meeting.

Shiela stood at the bottom of the stairs, watching the hatchway. Finally, Monica appeared, and they saw each other. Monica’s husband followed her, and they hugged a real 3-way.

The colonel walked past, “Shiela, I need a favor.” She looked at the three of them as they turned towards her. She had a shocked face, “Uh, let me guess. You two are related!”

They both nodded emphatically, but Lamar saw it too. “Holy crap!”

They both looked at him, “What?” they asked as if using one brain.

“It appears that your DNA,” pointing to Sheila, “is still in use on Earth in your family.” The colonel said, laughing.

A moment later, the cousins saw it. Lamar put his palm to his forehead, “Oh my god, there’s two of them!”

Sheila asked, “What was it you needed, Droid?”

“It can wait. You have a lot of catching up to do, most likely.” She looked at Lamar, “If they start driving you nuts, the bar is the building painted orange.” She smiled, “Always a good drink, and you can generally find someone to talk to about whatever is on your mind.”

“Thanks. I may just wander in there later.”

Sheila asked, “You be in the bar, Colonel?”

“Nope. I have an appointment at Romeo's house tonight. Peace, quiet, and just me.”

“Where is Romeo?”

“He is staying at Wilomena’s for a week. She is off the planet, and he needs to stay close to the action if needed!” She grinned, “Which means I get to play with his cats and dogs and enjoy the remote nothingness of his home.”

“Have fun!”

They waved to each other and parted in opposite directions.

~~~~~~~~~~~

Most of the inhabitants were gathered in Owl Square. Maybe 50% of the colony and 25% of the visitors. They were holding a welcome party, a picnic. In these numbers, this is the first time people from Earth have visited Terra – excluding military movements.
~~~~~~~~~~~

The rest of the groups were busy with assigned duties or roaming. Romeo was and has been working with Jack Deacon. Jack was Earth's foremost expert on the ARC and other communications technology. His family has lived in the city of Youngsville since the 20th century. Jack was Romeo and Wilomena's primary instructor before the colony ship launched. He was also the instructor for all the subsequent comms people for the other colony ships at the Youngsville complex after they all passed the introductory survival courses.

"I'll tell you, son, it is a bit odd. We were about the same age when you were in Youngsville. We hit a few of the bars together, I do believe." Jack said.

"We did. I remember it like it was yesterday." Romeo replied. Jack laughed because, in a way, it really did seem like yesterday for him, and he knew it.

"I'm now 30 years older than you, at least in appearance and possibly organic deterioration."

They laughed, "Interesting way to phrase it, Jack."

"We all reviewed everything you did to increase, improve, and expand the system. The smartest thing you did, and also the dumbest thing you did, was dropping the Rest Stop ARC on the BLUE channel." Jack grinned from ear to ear, "Mainly because the BLUE channel was reserved as a priority channel for emergency communications between here and Earth." He smiled again, "It also gave the people back home the backdoor access to your databases. All of them. When you processed the ARC to Rest Stop through

BLUE, they were pissed! I sat back and watched as did the other comms instructors. We even had popcorn."

"So, that was a way to spy on the colony, blue channel?"

"That it was. Now it's fixed. Using the Alliance comm sets, life is faster. The cloak and dagger boys had no way of gathering data covertly. So you closed that door; a job well done!"

Romeo stood there a moment, "What were they looking for?"

"Random shit, anger, dissent. Who knows. If you made personal logs or random thoughts, they had access to them too." Then, Jack changed the subject, "I want to see this comm setup that spans a few hundred kilometers. I understand you have a house somewhere outside of town that is fully connected?"

"I do. We can head there tomorrow mid-morning. I have a small shuttle we can use to get there, and it may take 25 minutes to travel. Several of us are going, and there is a need to move some equipment. I may bring a wall or two for the house if there's room."

Jack squinted his eye a bit and cocked his head, "So if it is a half-hour flight, why do you spend the night?"

"I will let you answer that at breakfast a few mornings from now." Romeo's turn to grin.

"OK, who is coming with us?" Jack asked.

Well, the shuttle holds eight; a pilot, a copilot, and six passengers. I'll be the copilot, and the Colonel will be the pilot; she loves to head out there even for one night. The others are you and Victoria, Wilomena, and Rich, and the last two on our little journey are two of our maintenance workers. We call them the Servants or the Handies. They need a few hours to upgrade some systems and run a few new cables you brought from Earth. So I can give them a hand to get it done faster. Of course, once the work is done, the rest of their time is spent on vacation. But, just so you know, everyone likes visiting my house." He paused, "Well, it is only a shelter at the moment, the biggest Adirondack you ever saw, but it does have running water," Romeo said.

"Hot and cold?"

"Yep, hot and cold."

"Nice.... So what's left to make it a paradise?"

"This trip, we are marking and setting the footers for the walls. They'll take a few days to set, so I'll return with the rest of the walls over the weekend and put them in place. I figure it will be a house in maybe three months or so. Before winter, for sure."

"We are slated to leave in ten days; if you need a hand, I would love to return with you."

"Excellent! You can even sign the plaque." Romeo said.

"What plaque?"

"In the main living area, I plan to put a plaque with the name of each person who contributed to the construction of the house, no matter how little or how much they worked. If they did anything, they helped. So I guess you'll be immortalized on my living room wall!" He looked at Jack, who just smiled at him.

"Interesting touch," Jack said. "Maybe we should head over to the picnic."

"We should, yes."

"Any idea what they are serving?" Jack asked.

"Cat burgers and sides, I think. Reminds me more of lamb than beef, but still pretty good food." They started walking toward Owl Square.

"So what's this new comm thing you mentioned? Sounds interesting."

Romeo said, "The Alliance has a way of having near instantaneous communications, and we found a way to adapt it to our communications array. I call it the Alliance Booster Module, but the real name of it is a long and hard-to-pronounce name in a language I cannot speak. However, when I asked them what the name meant, they told me communications booster module, so I got it." He smiled at that.

"Tomorrow, we can configure and run it to the downlink in orbit. Rest Stop has already installed theirs, and they said the clarity and throughput are amazing. They dropped off our link and are connected to Earth through the module. The delay is less than 3000 microseconds. A whole lot better than we have at the moment. When we are online, we can run a test with them. Once you get home, add it to the Earth array; data throughput will no longer be measurable, and voice and video will be instant. I was informed that the data throughput delay would be a whopping 15 milliseconds max. That's due to the processing of the circuitry in the box. They left me a dozen modules, so you can bring a few home with you. I figure you will want to take one apart and see what makes it tick." He took a long breath, "From what they tell me, only one is needed per planet. So, Earth, Mars, Jupiter Station, maybe the Moon. I can give you 6; if you need more, let me know. They give these things away like Halloween Candy. They believe communication is the key to minimizing conflict."

"Not a bad thought," Jack said.

Romeo nodded in agreement, "Yup, I agree."

Jack squinted, "How big is this thing?"

"Well, about as long as my forearm but a perfect cube. Weighs like 3 kilos, if I remember right. The exterior has a small display they set up for English, a series of connectors on 2 sides, as in input and output, and they are color-coded. Pink is in, and gray is out. A few buttons and that's about it. I opened one, and the inside was a black box. Wait till you see the circuit diagram, 43 pages."

"So, are their schematic symbols like ours?"

"Nope. I gave them a sheet of symbols and explanations. They created the circuit diagram using our symbols. They also said we would be better off once we understood their symbols. Beeker agrees." Romeo said. There was a little contempt in his voice as he mentioned Beeker. Jack noticed it but did not pursue it.

"Intriguing? I really wanna see the schematic for the unit."

“I have a copy of it for you in my office. We can review it after breakfast tomorrow.” Romeo told his old friend. Maybe I can make a printout, and we can look at it around the campfire at the house.” He continued as they walked, “The house may not be a house yet, but it does have a roof.” He grinned, “I am hungry!”

“Sounds like a plan. Let’s eat. I’m hungry, too. Seems like I ain’t et in half a lightyear.”

They walked to the Square, and as they approached the food area, the Colonel was there. She ended up in line with a few people before Jack and Romeo.

“Colonel. Got a sec.” She backed up in line to stand with them, “This is Jack Deacon. My comm instructor from the training center.”

“In Youngsville?”

“Yep,” Jack replied. “Were you a Captain when you were at the training center?”

A glimmer of memory surfaced, and Droid started remembering, “I was. Now I remember you. You taught me about colony comm units and reprogramming handy talkies. You were dating a young lady there at the time. She and I became friends and used to talk about you all the time. She was quite taken with you, and, may I say, she bragged about your dates.” She thought a moment, “What was her name, Veronica?”

“Victoria.” Jack blushed. She told him about the conversations she had had with Andrea. At that moment, fate was against Jack, and Veronica joined them.

“Hi, honey.” She looked around and saw Romeo, “You, I remember, but you, OH MY GOD, Andrea! It is wonderful to see you. I heard you were on a water planet or something.”

“No V, Rest Stop is my home. I am here this week in conference with the general. We want to increase our security teams and understand the new relationship with the Alliance.”

“That sounds heavy.” She replied.

“In a way. Now, tell me what I missed in the last 40.”

They started talking, and Romeo looked at Jack, “OK, we have officially lost those two.” Jack said and smiled, “So, how's the weather.” They laughed.

“Veronica.” It took a moment, but Romeo got her attention. “Just wanted you to know that the Colonel is joining us tomorrow on our trip. She likes it at my house. So you two will have a lot of time to talk.”

Now, they both got excited.

The line reached the food, and they each grabbed a plate. The women went to a table on the left, and Romeo and Jack went to a table on the right, several rows away. They sat and ate quietly.

Glancing at the Colonel and Veronica, somehow, they could eat and talk simultaneously.

Jack said, “How do they do that?”

Romeo replied, “I have no idea, but it would be an interesting case study.”

They looked at each other and nearly busted a gut.

CHAPTER TWELVE

Dayl Warrin took on the role of leader of the third settlement. He did not want to be the leader. He wanted the colony, his colony, and his leadership to be a committee. Each member of the settlement has a say in everything. In reality, they could never accomplish anything in their first few months. The committee, the meetings, the arguments, and the attitude led to more meetings, descent, and zero activities.

One of the new members stood at the last of all committee meetings and spoke, “Members of this committee. I did not come here from Rest Stop to argue. I did not come here to talk. I came here to live my life in a place with like-minded brothers and sisters, following the ideals, foresight, and vision of Dayl Warrin. He realized the colony was restrictive and thought hard about finding a solution, a resolution that attracted all of us.”

Michael Ross, a group member for almost two months, walked to the front of the gathering. He was loyal to the group and a very hard worker. He did things for others, not expecting anything in return. Everyone knew him and thought he was a great person. When he spoke, everyone listened. On top of that, he had the soul of a preacher and made his words fit into everyone's heart. What he said was understood by all.

Warrintown now has nearly 200 residents. Singles, roommates, and families. As he reached the front, he spoke a bit louder. “Friends. We need leadership. But leadership to lead is not what we are looking for. We are at an impasse. We cannot move forward because some of you want yes, some want no, and others want whatever. We need a way to get past this, and I propose that Dayl, our visionary, become our group's leader. Yes, he can decide for us for the good of the settlement, but at the same time, he will enact the will of the group.”

He walked to Dayl and put a hand on his shoulder. Dayl was sitting quietly at the end of the table in front of the room. “I am going to make a motion. I want you to listen to this motion and consider what it means for our future.” He paused a heartbeat or two for punctuation, “ALL YE HEAR, I make a motion that Dayl Warrin be named our duly elected Mayor of Warrintown with the ability to make decisions for the good of the group, our future and to represent us at the Terra leadership meetings.”

It was silent for a moment, then a voice from the back of the room, “I SECOND THAT MOTION!”

“We will vote in a moment. Think about your answer. Yea, or Nay. Yes or no. There is no in-between, no maybe, no whatever.”

Michael paused momentarily, “All in favor of naming Dayl Warrin our Mayor as stated previously, signify by saying YEA.”

It echoed in the room. The sound was louder than anything they had heard in a long time. "All opposed signify by saying NAY."

One woman in the back of the room said nay. She was the only one. Michael continued, "The yea's had it, but there is one nay. I assume you would like a discussion."

"I would." She stood and spoke, "Dayls knowledge, vision, and abilities are not in question. I feel that he can accomplish great things for this settlement. Still, I propose, no, I make a motion that Michael Ross, you young man, be given the title of assistant Mayor or Town manager or whatever we decide with the sole responsibility of advising, being a sounding board, and when appropriate, playing the role of Devils Advocate to the Mayor."

As she finished, half the room seconded the motion. "All in favor?"

The yeas thundered through the room. "All opposed," The room was so silent you could hear nothing but breathing.

Dayl stood, "Michael, if you accept this role, I shall also. Then, we can present ourselves to the meeting tomorrow in Columbus and take our place on the leadership team for this planet."

Michael shook his head. He did not want to be a leader. He was a technician, a fixer. He did not want to be responsible for all these lives he was looking at. The crowd of people, community members of the town. His new brothers and sisters. He stared at Dayl for a long second, "I accept." He said to Dayl. Loud enough for all to hear.

Dayl grabbed Michael in a bear hug, and the crowd erupted. The settlement was becoming a town. They trade with their neighbors and are happy to accept visitors. They tell them that if they come for a vacation, it is a no-frills stay. You get a room and food, can walk around, and enjoy the sights. You are also expected to take part in communal work and activities. Planting, sowing, reaping, and harvesting of produce. Building new structures or whatever else may be available when you arrive.

Alliance members find this a refreshing and relaxing vacation. Working in the dirt, blanching and preserving produce, and building. The residents are mainly from Terra. However, several are from Rest Stop, and a few from Earth were granted permission to migrate to the colony.

The community is very beautiful. The gardens, the parks, and the trails all interconnect. People from all over the Alliance travel here to relax. There are no hotels, no barracks. It is a place where you can come, set up your own residence as a campsite, and relax. Several buildings are available if necessary, and they do not recommend a winter stay in a tent.

Romeo has been there a few times. He stays in the central area when he comes out to do a comm install or an upgrade. His last trip lasted two weeks, and he and Rebekka made a second honeymoon out of it.

He was there to work, somewhat. He added remote comm units so those in tents, cabins, and temporary structures could have a good signal and call home if needed. This also is mobile, meaning a visitor can call home and walk around to show off the town area, activities, and people. Michael thought of this to increase visitors and free advertising.

The connection to the Alliance comm network is complete. Meaning you can make a call to anyone in the universe at your convenience. At first, the residents of Warrintown were paranoid that they were being spied on and did not want a comm system installed. But after it saved a few lives, they realized it was necessary.

Romeo gave people a few HTs and told them to use them in an emergency. A few weeks later, a woman, Priya Kaur Bhullar, fell from a roof she was assembling, and Michael called Columbus Medical for assistance. They were there in 15 minutes. The doctor was thankful they did not move her but kept her comfortable. Finally, they could scoop her up and take her to medical, and her mate went with her.

She had cracked her spine, and Ralph was able to fix it during a 7-hour surgery. Ralph poked a sharp point on her toes a few hours after the surgery, but there was no reaction. He commented it may be too soon. We will check in the morning.

The following day, he entered her room. As she woke up, she instinctively moved her legs. Ralph started crying. She was going to be okay.

"How's the pain?" He asked her.

She was lying flat on her back. "It hurts, but not terrible. Will I be able to walk?"

“Considering that as you woke, you shuffled your legs without thinking, which means I managed to put everything back where it belongs.”

“How long was the surgery?” She asked.

Robbie Kizinski, her mate, answered, “Seven-long-grueling-hours!”

Ralph laughed. He slapped Robbie on the back, “Seemed a lot longer to me, son.”

Robbie hugged Ralph, “As soon as I can stand, I owe you one or two of those myself.” Priya said to Ralph.

As did Robbie, Priya fully recovered and went to Columbus Medical for training as an EMT. They decided they needed medical services to be close by in case something happened. So they were the first to complete the training from Warrintown.

The settlement Mayor asked if they could install a full communications array and train a few people to maintain it. Romeo and his team showed the Warrintown communication team everything about the systems. After a while, for several years, they all fell into a peaceful rhythm of coexistence.

Granted, until the rhythm was realized, there were brawls, fights, animosity, and hard feelings on both sides of the fence. One side did not understand why they left the colony, and the other could not understand how they could stay. But, finally, they understood, and the issues smoothed out and disappeared.

The primary product of Warrintown is produce. They are amazing farmers and experts in genetic splicing to increase production and change it to create a new, usually tasty, version of itself.

The creator can name it whatever they want; a few names are unique, like the sweet root. Combining a Russett potato and a yam with celery root created a unique purple vegetable the size of a watermelon. The texture is the same as any tuber, and the flavor is sweet. It can be eaten happily in its raw form, roasted and boiled. The base protein is more than any legume they have on the planet, and the plant grows, from planting to harvest, in a little over a month. It is a hit in the Alliance, and Terra has become known for relaxing, eating, and farming. All of Terra is proud of this fact, and all five settlements work together.

The two newest settlements are located at Westing Lake and are considered resorts. Several younger residents who started in the restaurant opened them with diverse interests. One is called WATER, and the other is named BEACH.

The Water resort is underwater. Rooms and facilities are encased in transparent material from an Alliance world, Praxit, which is industrial and creative. The Alliance assisted in cleaning up the lake and removing the impurities so the water was safe. An ionized asteroid landed in the lake a long time ago. The odd impurity they first discovered was the chemical result of the radioactive asteroid, about 50 meters in diameter. Their assistance in detecting and removing it made the water clean.

Once the water was cleaned, the lake flourished, and life expanded. When they discovered the impurity was radiation, some joked about a fish with two tails or six eyes.

~~~~~~~~~~~

Romeo woke up early this morning. He decided to go out and sit on his deck and watch the sunrise. Something he has not done in a while. He brought his favorite chair to the edge of the deck. Propping his feet on the railing but not high enough to block the rising star, he rested comfortably in his chair, sipping a cup of Rest Stop coffee. It really is good and puts the exclamation point on a beautiful sunrise.

Romeo is a creature of habit. He sets the coffee up the night before, knowing when he wants to wake up. Then, as he wakes, he smells the coffee and gets up.

He's looking at the horizon and can begin to notice trees start to form in the gaining light and rocks that he knows are there. He sees ripples on the lake as a fish jumps out of the water. He always wondered why the fish do that but has never asked or decided to find out. Perhaps the fish is being pursued by a larger and hungrier fish, and it is a way of finding a safe haven? He may look into it one day, but not today.

His wife, Rebekka, walked onto the deck carrying her coffee, sat beside him, and joined him without saying anything. She laid her legs on top of his, and both were content. They just sit there and watch the sun come up. They face the rising star directly, and it hits them full in the face. Battling the star as it rises, they fight. Keeping their
~~~~~~~~~~~

eyes open as long as possible. Eventually, they allow the sun to win, at least today.

The beauty and majesty of sunrise are a mystery and a religious experience to some people. Romeo and Rebekka included. There's absolute silence. Not even the wind is making noise at the moment. Ripples on the lake can be seen clearly for some reason. The swells seemed to be going in the opposite direction of normal, but that may be an illusion created by the gaining light. Finally, his favorite tree comes into view. The tree is maybe 40 meters tall and a meter and a half in diameter at its base. All the leaves are facing the gaining sunlight, and all branches from the tree's opposite side have come around to greet the light this morning. They sit there and enjoy the light as it approaches their body and warms them in a way that nothing else can; they hold hands and just sit. Unaware, but aware, of the gaining light.

Colonel Droid was standing behind them most of this time. She also appreciates a perfect sunrise such as this. She also enjoyed the coffee and appreciated that it awaited her when she entered the kitchen. After all, she brought Romeo and Rebekka this current shipment of coffee from Rest Stop. It is where she lives most of the time.

She makes a comment to Romeo. "Well, you guys are great hosts. This has been the best vacation I've had in a long time. I will make you breakfast this morning to thank you for the respite."

Romeo begins to speak, but his wife cuts him off, "Have at it. If you need any help, let me know."

Droid smiled and went back into the house.

Romeo looked at his wife. "Looks like we have one hell of a downstairs maid."

From in the kitchen, "I heard that!"

~~~~~~~~~~~

Droid dressed in her 'uniform' and walked into the living room. "Well, it's been a good vacation. But I need to get back to reality."

"Been nice having you here," Rebekka said.

"Thanks. Always great hanging out with you." She smiled at Romeo, "Him too, I guess." She winked at him.

Lieutenant Commander Marcus Reyez walked into the room. On Terra, there are maybe five people named Marcus. One afternoon, all of them were having lunch together. Droid walked over to the table, and all they did was look at her. She went and sat with Romeo. He commented he had the same experience. They all had a good laugh, but a 'Marcus' club? Really

Droid spoke, "Wow. Navy people take so long to get dressed."

Marcus grinned, "That would be your fault." He looked at his fiance, "Over and over and over."

Romeo spoke, "Marcus, I hear that the Alliance has a drug that makes transitioning from our gravity to her gravity much easier. Still takes a few weeks, but do you think you'll be headed there to test the theory?"
~~~~~~~~~~~

"I considered it, but Droid shut it down. She said one in 8 still has negative effects. However, one of the worlds in the Alliance has developed a promising gene therapy."

Rebekka jumped in, "The Dreelin. I heard about that. Their world is the same gravity as ours, and I am scheduled to head there in a week to see if there are any red flags for humans."

"How long will you be there?" Droid asked.

"A few days. Not more than five days, I suppose. Why?"

"Well, I need to head there for a five-day weapons seminar. So I can drop by here and pick you up, and we can head there together."

Rebekka grinned, "A girl's week off planet!" Then, she laughed, "When are you headed there?"

"In 15 days," Droid replied.

"Sounds like a plan. However, scheduling the shuttle to pick me up and bring me home is a pain in the gluteus maximus. So what will you be flying?"

"Well, it is a weapons seminar, and my attack craft is due for an upgrade or two, so how would you like to fly in an attack fighter?"

"OH, HELL YEA!" Rebekka said. Droid cracked up. "Think I could take the stick for a little?"

"It may be arranged." She looked at her lover, "We need to go. I have a meeting at the spaceport in an hour, then I need to head home. This gravity is great, but I must reacclimate to my normal gravity, or it will be bad."

"Meeting?" Romeo asked.

"Yep, about the weapons trip, actually. Marcus is coordinating your end, so I will tell him about the two of us." She smiled an evil grin and turned toward LtCmdr Marcus, "Honey, please coordinate the time on the planet for the weapon upgrade to coincide with Rebekka's trip."

"Yes, dear," he responded, and Romeo almost spit out the coffee he was drinking.

"Unfortunately, I am not attending the meeting. I will be linked by comm though during the meetings." He turned to Droid and winked, "My role is simple." Marcus said, "Provide planning and coordination for the ships looking to add or upgrade weapons technology to their vessels. The work will be accomplished in the geosynchronous orbit of Terra, each taking about two weeks to complete. Smaller ships will land and be upgraded at the far end of the Spaceport. In addition, the newest barracks are held for the crews of those ships, and we suspect it will significantly boost the colony."

"AH! Now I understand why we needed to upgrade the comms in all those rooms. A couple of the rooms have encrypted setups, too. I'm guessing the captain and first officer's quarters?"

Marcus looked severe, "Good guess. But please never mention either of those two statements again."

"Mention what?" Romeo said.

"No clue," Marcus answered.

"We need to fly. I need more coffee before the meeting. Maybe a slice of cheesecake, too." Droid said.

She has not used her real first name since she met the Alliance leader all those years ago. Andrea, a beautiful human name for an attractive human woman, is also the word in the language of another world for a toilet. Calling someone Colonel Toilet or Colonel Toilet Battle brings on a vision that, well, just did not seem right. Her nametag even said Colonel 'DROID' Battle. The new nametag was delivered from Earth quite a while ago. Command permitted her to go by her nickname for planetary peace and tranquility. It made for an exciting discussion when Marzo first visited Earth, and a few of the human team members had the name Andrea.

When she met in groups or spoke to crowds, she mentioned that Droid was a name her friends and leaders gave her nearly half a century ago. Then she tells them her real first name and waits for or allows the smiles and chuckles. She tells them it's OK to laugh. In my world, she tells them, it is a good name. The name is from my maternal lineage. A word that my mother proudly gave to me. In her home world, Earth, Andrea means WARRIOR or PROTECTOR. Andrea is a beautiful, royal, and strong name with positive connotations like courage, bravery, and strength.

Once the laughter subsides, she introduces her mother. Major Brenda Battle, also known as Brendar the Barbarian. More laughter from those attending, and the ice….is effectively broken. The proceedings always move smoothly after that, and the results are more than expected.

Colonel Droid is quite a diplomat. She is also an accomplished speaker.

CHAPTER THIRTEEN

For the past few decades, the colonies have grown, made names for themselves, and become destinations within the Alliance.

Since day one, Marzo Nuteq has been the Alliance's leader and Droid's close friend. They often vacation together in places most people would not consider a vacation destination.

When Earth decided to promote Colonel Andrea Battle to the rank of general, they chose to do so uniquely, using her dear friend as a means to an end.

RING

“Hi, Nuteq. I love it when you call.” Andrea said as she answered her comm.

“My dear friend, I need your assistance with a little problem on the Alliance capital. Do you think you can break away for a few days?” Marzo Nuteq said as she lured Droid to the planet as discreetly as possible.

“I think I can. When do you need me on Marenga?”

“Three days would be perfect. You can stay in the presidential palace. You, your husband, your parents, and your children." She paused a moment, "How are my babies?"

"Wix and Malaxi are fine; they hear you asking about them."

"Wonderful. I am so happy that Strength and Smart are doing well. I have an offer for them for their future careers. Malaxi has an appointment at the secondary educational facility here on Marenga if she wants to accept it. With her basic understanding of astrophysics and mathematics, the school has a great position for her to learn." She paused a moment, "Now Wix is another story. He likes fighting, weapons, tactics, and fighting. Did I mention fighting?" She laughed in her way, "He is so you and your mother. There is a program here to train young people for protective services. Since Earth has joined the Alliance in all respects, training for military service is accomplished all over the universe. The program here trains officers, leadership, and special tactics."

"They are excited now. You realize I may have to stay there on the planet if they are there?" Droid mentioned.

"Your room in my residence is always available for you."

"Thank you, my friend. See you in a few days. All of us." She thought momentarily, and Droid asked, "Is there anything you need me to bring you from here?"

Nuteq smiled over the comm, "Actually, there is if it is not too much trouble. I would love for this to be a leadership meeting at least a little bit of the time. So can you see that the Earth, Rest Stop, and Terra leaders come with you also?"

"It's getting pretty crowded in my shuttle as it is?"

"I will send the Serenity, and you can stop to pick everyone up. The leadership of all Alliance worlds will be on the planet, and we can convene a special meeting."

"Sounds like fun. Serenity as a taxi service." Droid smiled.

"What? I know that grin." Nuteq said.

Andrea said, "Can I drive?"

~~~~~~~~~~

Marzo Nuteq sat in her seat on the dais of the meeting place. She looked around the room. Hundreds of people are talking, hugging, and being their best version. Nuteq loved these moments. For her, this is what it was all about. The Alliance. As a group, no one is better than the next. No planet is more important than another. All people are one, and all people are equal. Each world, people, and culture contribute to the whole, which is beautiful.

The room was filled with hundreds of people of all colors, shapes, sizes, and appearances. An entire section of humans was close to the front, with the Earth President in the front row.

Marzo Nuteq nodded to the Earth president, and she walked to the podium. As she did, the room quieted. This is out of the ordinary as precedence, and everyone was curious.

"Thank you, my friends. Your invitation to this meeting is a time to elect a replacement to the second in command of the Alliance." She turned to Marzo. "This committee has taken your recommendation and unanimously approved your
~~~~~~~~~~

replacement for Marti Tawna. However, before the replacement is announced, I would like to call Colonel Battle up before this assembly."

Andrea stood and walked to the President. She wore her sword, as did Nuteq, and it clattered a bit as she walked. However, most believe both of them allowed it to rattle on purpose. They did love the attention.

Standing at attention at the side of the Earth President, she saluted. "President Marlow, it is my pleasure to report to you."

"I hope you feel that way 10 minutes from now?" The President grinned, and Andrea looked curious at her leader.

"Colonel Droid Battle," Careful to avoid her real name because it always elicits chuckles from the audience, "I called you up here for a two-fold purpose. I will inform you about point one, and Marzo Nuteq will inform you about the second."

"OK?" Droid answered in more of a question.

"You have been a Colonel for nearly two decades and accomplished much. Therefore, Earth Services is promoting you to the permanent rank of General. Congratulations,. General Battle."

The room roared, and with everyone there and nearly everyone familiar with her in one form or another, no one was quiet.

Her parents came out to hug her, and the President quieted the room. "Lieutenant Colonel Brenda Battle and

Lieutenant Colonel Kathy Battle. I am so happy you are here. Save me some time."

Brenda said, "Uh oh." She looked at Kathy. They knew what was about to happen. At the exact same moment, they planted their face into their palm. Took a moment, then returned to the position of attention.

Droid smiled.

"With the promotion of your daughter," The President said, "that leaves a hole in several places. For one, Rest Stop and the training facility. Therefore, you are both promoted to Colonel, with Brenda as the new leader of the training center on Rest stop and Kathy as the new tactical officer of the Alliance fleet."

The applause started again. This time, Nuteq stood, and the room quieted.

"My cabinet both enjoys and endures, the two of you in most cases, but the main reason you were chosen for these assignments are your creativity, unique perspective, and the fact that you would only occupy one cabin when you travel." She laughed, "Seriously, the cabinet realized that humans were strategists. But, Colonel K, you, above all humans' possess the most twisted and devious mind."

Kathy saluted, "Thank you, Marzo."

"My friends, I truly adore my role as leader of the Alliance, and I hope I accomplish what you need me to do for you." The room applauded. "Thank you, but my dear friend, for all these years, is stepping down to move into a quieter life. He wants to travel more for fun. But he and I decided his replacement needs to be someone we all know. Also, the person needs to be someone I can speak plainly to and with all our best interests in mind daily." She paused, and Andrea started to get a weird feeling. She closed her eyes slowly and almost imperceptibly shook her head as if it would change the following sentence.

"General Battle, Andrea," Small chuckles are always expected, "Droid. I am honored to inform you that everyone in this room voted for and approved you as my new second. That would be the position of Marzi."

The room applauded, and Andrea raised her hand. The room quieted. Andrea walked to the podium so the microphone would hear her voice clearly.

"Marzo, Madame President, leaders of the Alliance, I accept under one condition." She looked at Marzo and said, "You must all let me know if I do anything stupid!"

Everyone in the room yelled, "Agreed!"

The Earth President stood. "Marzi!" The room quieted, "I am honored to inform you that your retirement from the Earth Forces began 11 hours ago. Midnight, June 1 in Seattle, Washington." This is where the new Pentagon was established after Yellowstone. "Earth Command would like to thank you for nearly half a century of service on multiple planets and solar systems, and we all," waving her hands to the members of the Alliance in the room, "look forward to the great thing we expect from you in the future as the second in command of the Alliance."

Barely close enough to be picked up by the mic, Brenda and Kathy said simultaneously, “Oh dear lord, we’re doomed!” Everyone laughed.

Since joining the Alliance, humans have injected humor, fun, excitement, and a new eye into all aspects of the Alliance. More and more humans are taking leadership roles, and not one is doing this out of ego. On the contrary, they genuinely want to help.

The rest of the day was a party reception, and Marti Droid saw her new office. Her family was with her.

CHAPTER FOURTEEN

“Marti, we have arrived in the Earth's planetary system.” The comm erupted with the information.

Marti Droid, Andrea Battle, stood at the window of her stateroom aboard her starship, sipping a cup of coffee and daydreaming. “Thank you.” She said into the air. “I will be on the bridge in a moment.”

She turned and finished dressing. She placed the sword in her scabbard before the full-length mirror and smiled from one side of her mouth. A long, slow, satisfying smile. Perhaps a grin, possibly a smirk.

She left her cabin, walked a few steps to the left, and then toward the bridge. She stopped. Pressing the bell and waiting for the door to slide open.

“Enter.” The door opened, and she entered the room.

“Marzo. We are here.”

“I am aware, my friend.” She looked at Droid, “Good, you are properly attired.” Glancing at her sword. She placed her sword close to correct on her waist, as she had been doing all these years.

“Marzo, after all this time, you have not learned.” She smiled, “Perhaps you miss-wear the sword to make me crazy.”

“Possibly a little of both!” Marzo Nuteq replied and laughed.

“There! Now we can meet the Earth delegation.” They both stood in front of the mirror and looked at themselves and each other. They wore similar garments, their version of a uniform. “DAMN! We are hot!” They both laughed.

For the past two decades, Andrea and Nuteq have led the Alliance. They did not do it alone. They had a lot of help, some from Earth, Terra, and Rest Stop, and multiple people from various planets associated with the Alliance.

Marzo Nuteq has been the leader for 36 years, and Droid has been her Marti, vice leader, and 2nd leader for 23. They have expanded the Alliance into a large number of 56 distinct species. All but one were oxygen breathers, but that one species could breathe an Alliance atmosphere briefly.

Some worlds were light gravity, others were not. Rest Stop was closer to the midpoint. When visiting the high gravity, three standard gravities, it took its toll on anyone. Medicine has found quick ways to allow for an increase in gravity. Although vacationing in those worlds was delicate, moving to them posed a unique set of problems.

Travel, starships, shuttles, ground transport, and hover vehicles have significantly changed. For example, the scheduled shuttle's travel time from Terra to Rest Stop was less than an hour. To the Alliance capital or to Earth was four days from Terra, and a direct flight would take just under seven days. The shuttle from the Alliance capital made weekly runs to Earth, with a one-day stopover at Terra. Same for the return flight.

Beeker transports connected the Alliance like it had never been connected before. The universe was smaller now. There were standard flights from and to many points within the Alliance. Trust and friendship led the way between many worlds. But, all were not roses and glitter in the universe, unfortunately. Some factions sought to destroy what the Alliance stood for.

Wix and Malaxi were both off the planet, traveling for their positions. However, they each became top in their field as Malaxi is a very proficient instructor at the university and a roving instructor to many worlds, including Earth.

Her brother, Wix, made it his life's goal to learn every fighting style in all Alliance worlds. So he trained many instructors in as many as they could remember, and together, that team taught the military of the Alliance. They prepared for a time they hoped would never come.

The exploration ships were happy they were aboard as they found a new species and were instantly attacked. The ship was boarded, and the team halted the attack as it began. Sending the attackers back to their ship, where they disconnected and ran.

The species, the Maronz, were ruthless. They strived for conquest, battle, and taking what they wanted. What they wanted was whatever they saw. They had an alliance of sorts as well. A dark army, where attacking, killing, and taking was the end goal.

Wix and his team of instructors had their work cut out '**To Train and To Win**.' Their motto. Droid sat in on a few classes, and some cadets were slow to spar with the Marzi. Finally, Wix took her on, and the first time he threw his mother, the class let out a collected gasp.

Droid looked at him after she stood up, of course, and said, "That was cool. Teach it to me." So he did, and after a half hour of practice, she mastered the throw and tossed him across the room. The students all cheered for her.

As he stood, "Oh sure. Cheer for the Marzi because she tossed her poor young son like a dish rag." The cheers got louder. "At least I know where I stand in the room."

She always made it a point to come to one of the first classes of a new session. Yes, she was Marzi, but FIRST and foremost, she was a soldier, a diplomat, a member of the Alliance, a wife, and a mother. She wanted it clear that NO ONE in the Alliance is more special than any other. Wix never disappoints. She always ends up on her ass and then tells him to teach the move to her.

The next time she shows up in that class, the others understand she really wants to learn. And she always does.

This class was different.

Droid stood up after being knocked on her ass by her son again, but this time, instead of requesting instruction, she secured the room.

"Wix, how is this class?" She asked.

"Well, Mom-Zi," The class always laughed when he called her that, "of the classes in the past year, this group has picked up more in a shorter time."

She dropped her head and thought momentarily, Looking up at the 20 in the room, "I need a team. About 20 people and a leader. Do you all understand the word covert?"

Nods from everyone.

"Good. The Maronz are on the move and really pissing me off. Several years ago, I captured one of their ships, and we made a few modifications, giving us an advantage. This is the Trojan Horse." She looked around and asked, "Does anyone not understand the Trojan Horse reference?" No one raised a hand, "Good. We must land on their world, infiltrate their command center, and take as much as possible. We do not care what we take. We just want to take all that we can. They revel in the fact they take and take, and no one stands up to them. That needs to change. The goal is to let them know we can and will protect ourselves." She looked at their faces. "The secondary goal is to plant a program to monitor activities. Who here is a tech wiz?"

One young female raised a hand. "Please join us here."

"Yes, Marzi."

"And stop that!" Droid said, "In a place like this, all of you can call me Droid." She looked at her son, "You, well, whatever."

The room chuckled again. She looked at Wix. "Kiddo, is she trained, I mean fully trained?"

"She is Droid-Zi."

She stopped dead in her tracks and looked at him, “New one?” She said.

“I thought it up just now and took it for a test flight. What Cha Think?”

“Not one of your best, but not bad.” Andrea continued, “What is your name?” She said, looking at the young lady.

“Captain Marcee.” The young lady replied.

“You look human. Are you from Earth?”

“My mother is human. My father is Sarutan.”

“Interesting. That means you have a denser cellular structure?”

“Yes, Ma’am….I mean Droid.”

“Perfect. As a matter of fact, I need to send you to Saruta for a week to get familiar with Maronz tech. Do you have any family there? Any romantic interests where you can show off to not arouse suspicion?”

Wix spoke, “Well, that is an interesting question, Mom.”

“MOM! You have not called me Mom since you last got into trouble in school.” Then, she thought for a moment, “Wait? You two?”

They both nodded. Droid smiled, “Well then, one question. Is it serious?”

Wix said, “Last night, she said yes. So I was going to tell you at dinner.”

“WONDERFUL! You can tell your Grannies at dinner, and I will act surprised.” She looked at Marcee, “As for you!

You have permission to call me Mom-Zi!" She hugged her, "Welcome to my nightmare of a family!"

The rest of the class just stood there. When they hugged, they all approached and hugged the new couple. Once it returned to a quiet place, "OK, you need to learn the systems, and you can take THAT…." She points at her son, "With you to show off to your family. Does anyone in your family know your future spouse is my little baby?" She shook her head and looked at Wix, "You really need to tell me their reaction when they find out who your amazing and impressive Mother is," She looked at the class, "Am I right?" They all agreed. "And you need to tell them when you get back."

She changed modes like she flipped a switch. Everyone was used to it by now and fell into the new tone with her.

"The Maronz were attacking more frequently and damaging Alliance ships. Each transport had a security flight assigned. Each security flight was a set of four fighter craft flying a diamond formation above, below, and on either side of the transport. The fighters deterred the attacks, but they needed more. We need them to understand that if they encroached on the Alliance, the Alliance would stop them." She turned to Wix, "Captain Wix. You are promoted to Major and will lead this mission. Your direct commander will be Colonel Rosta, who will provide you with the details on Saruta. Who is your second in command?"

"My Fiance!"

"Really? Perfect! Captain Marcee, you are promoted to Major and the 'T' flight leader. Let me or the Grannies know if there are any internal position changes in the team, and we will make the changes for you. Granny B will ensure you are all up to speed on the newest weapons, still classified, and some really cool shit you will play with; Granny K will provide tactics and tech."

They all knew who Granny B and K were. They retired from active military service and took positions of advisement in the Alliance. Both now reside at Rest Stop but have their shuttle for trips wherever needed.

As if on queue, they entered the room.

"Mom's. How did you enter a room that was sealed." Droid asked.

K quickly replied, "Clean living."

B said, "Kid, we wrote the protocols to seal the room. So if we want to enter, it lets us."

Wix looked at his Mom, "Mom-Zi, we may need to look into that." The room let out a collective chuckle.

Droid said, "Before we start, B has something."

"Wix, here is your Majors rank." Kathy removed the captain's insignia, and Brenda pinned the Major's rank on him. "Who is your second,"

Wix pointed to Marcee. "I remember you. You and Wix had lunch with us a few weeks ago. Congratulations, Captain, you are now a Major."

Droid spoke, "She is also going to Saruta for training. She has family there."

“Is she traveling alone?” K asked. She knew…..

Wix spoke, “OK, Grannies, you seem to already know. Marcee and I are engaged and headed to Saruta to introduce me to her family.”

“Oh my god, that is wonderful!” Droid said.

Momma B looked at her, “Bullshit, and by the way, you need acting lessons.” Then, she looked at the class, “How long has she known?”

One really tall guy raised his hand, “Maybe five minutes.”

“I like this guy. Do you like blowing shit up?” He nodded emphatically, as did the guy next to him. “Perfect, you two report to me on the range tomorrow. We can teach you the new weapons, and you can teach the others.”

It got quiet again, and B started, “OK. This briefing is classified Alliance secret.” She began the briefing.

CHAPTER FIFTEEN

It was a 19-hour flight by scheduled shuttle, but since Wix is Wix, he could borrow an attack craft to bring to Saruta. They had a few upgrades they needed to test, and the attack craft was to be the prototype. If it all works well, the new weapons will improve their capabilities in a firefight.

It did extend the flight to almost two and a half days, but it gave them a chance to talk about themselves, their future, and their families.

"Alliance Attack Craft, this is Saruta Spaceport Control. You are cleared for a straight-in approach to the testing center. Please identify the lifeforms on the craft."

Marcee recognized the voice. It was one of her childhood classmates. "Maretta, this is Major Marcee of the Alliance Protectorate. I am in command of this ship. My second is Major Wix."

Everyone knew the name Wix.

"Major Marcee, did you say Wix was your second?"

Wix spoke, "Her home planet. I put her in command of this trip." Then, he paused, "By the way, this is Wix."

When the controller spoke, they heard laughter, “Major, I mean Majors. Welcome to Saruta, and I hope we can meet for a drink or dinner while you are here.”

Marcee said, “It’s a date. Name the time and place; the Major here will put it into our schedule.”

“Agreed. Where are you staying?”

“My mother's house.”

“Oh boy, does she know who the houseguest is to be?”

“Not a clue, and let’s keep it that way, please.”

“Marcee, you are mean, but I need to hear everything over dinner.”

“You got it. Bring your husband to the dinner. It will be fun.”

“Agreed.” She paused, “You will hit the atmosphere in 19 seconds. Once you do, make your way to the testing field. Local transport is waiting for your arrival.” She paused, “The driver is Winsin Markk.”

“Excellent!” She looked at Wix, “We dated briefly. Thankfully, he ended up marrying my sister. They are perfect together. You’ll meet him when we land and her at dinner tonight.”

Wix took a deep breath, let it out slowly, and said, “This is going to be a fascinating dinner.”

From the comm, “It certainly will be. Have fun. Spaceport out!”

They looked at each other, smiled, kissed, and readjusted in their seats. “Strap in,” Marcee said. “Orbital control. We touched the atmosphere. Proceeding to test center as scheduled.”

~~~~~~~~~~~

The landing went smoothly; Marcee is an excellent pilot, and Wix is, too. A transport pulled up as they shut down the systems and put the ship to sleep.

“Marcee dear, our ride is here,” Wix said. Taking half a step outside the exit, “Hi, Winsin.”

The look on his face was priceless. “Do I know you?”

Wix grinned, “Not yet!” At that moment, Marcee popped into the doorway.

“Winsin, have you met my future husband?” Marcee said in a very jovial, almost joking manner.

“No. Hi, I’m Winsin Markk. Marcee and I have known each other most of our lives.” Then, he paused momentarily, “I’m here to give you a ride wherever you want.”

“That is excellent. My name is Wix Battle. Marcee and I are engaged to be married.”

Marcee said, “Do you remember my mother's house?”

“Yep.”

“Great. Take us there, please.”

“Sure thing. Got any bags we need to bring with us?”

“Just these,” Wix said as he picked up a couple of small duffles.
~~~~~~~~~~~

"Perfect, toss them in the back, and we can head to her mom's house." Winsin stopped dead in his tracks, "Wix Battle! As in the son of the Marzi?"

"Wow, great memory. Yep, that's my Mom."

"Sorry, sir," Winsin said, looking like he saw a ghost.

"Do that shit again, and I will personally beat the crap out of you. My Mom is my Mom. I am just the guy who plans to marry this amazing woman. So, treat me like a friend, and we will get along splendidly."

Winsin smiled, "May I make an observation?"

"Please do," Marcee said.

"We have received reports that the family members of the Marzi are not power hungry, nor are they ego maniacs. On the contrary, they are people like anyone else. Nothing special, nothing that needs to be amplified or ceremonialized."

"And?" Wix said.

"I like it. Wanna stop off for a beer?"

Marcee and Wix gave huge grins and said simultaneously, "DEFINITELY!"

About fifteen minutes later, they stopped at a pub. Winsin got out, as did Marcee and Wix. They went into the pub and sat at a table. As Winsin sat, he looked at the bartender and held up a thumb and two fingers. A few minutes later, a young lady walked over with three mugs. She set them in front of them one at a time and stared at Wix for a moment too long as if trying to remember his name.

No one said anything in the process. She returned to the bar and tapped a few keys on a screen. Then, pointed at the screen and looked back at Wix.

Wix stood. Looked at the bar and at Winsin, "Need to squash this now, and fast."

He walked over to the bar and stood next to the server. "Hello, my name is Wix. Marcee and I are to be married soon, and I like tipping a server and a bartender who understands what I am telling them." They both stood there transfixed on Wix, more impressed by who he was instead of the fact he was there and acting like a natural person.

Wix continued, "Please allow me to say this one time only. You obviously know who I am and, most likely, my mom. Still, in this place," He looked around, realizing they were the only patrons, "You can call me whatever you want. If no one recognizes me when I am here, make up a name, Roger, for example. I have no interest in being known as HIM, Her Son, or whatever. Feed me beers like that, and if you have some excellent Earth Scotch, I will definitely be your friend. Marcee and I will be married in town in a few months. We will be looking for a place for the dinners, staff for the wedding, and many other things."

The bartender extended a hand. "Hello Roger, my name is Jeramie. This is Greta. She and I are married, and we own this place. You like Earth Scotch," He reached behind him, not even looking, grabbed a bottle, and poured a shot, "Try this!"

Wix picked up the glass and downed it in one gulp. "Holy shit, that is fantastic."

“Got it from a guy who was down on his luck. Cost me a pretty penny, too.” He grinned, “Expensive too. Want another?”

“Definitely, and one for each of us,” Wix smiled at him, “Pour yourself one too.” He looked at Greta.

“No, thank you, but thanks. In 7 months, I’ll be able to have a drink again, but till then, water, juice, and more water.”

“Jeramie, you keep this and hold it till she is ready. Then, when she is, the two of you drink a toast to Marcee, me, my mom, whoever.”

Jeramie smiled and slapped Wix on the shoulder. Then, taken aback at the solidity, “Damn boy, you are solid!” He caught himself and continued, “You got it, my friend. Now, you hungry?"

"Not really.” He smiled and tapped the tiny glass; Jeramie got the idea and topped it off. “Dinner with the future family tonight, and before you ask, they have no clue who Marcee will marry.”

“Mate, may I say you are one odd duck?”

Wix smiled, “Yep!”

Jeramie laughed, “Then, my friend, you are one odd duck.” They tapped their shot glasses and downed them.

Wix returned to the table, and a moment later, Greta gave them all a shot.

“Thanks, Greta,” Wix said.

Marcee joked, “Do I need to be worried?”

Greta said, "No, dear. Roger here is an old family friend of my husband." She started laughing as she went back to the bar.

"WHAT?" Winsin and Marcee said together.

Wix laughed as he explained the conversation and that Greta was about 2 months pregnant. "This is the best scotch I ever had." He picked up his glass, as did the other two, and said, "To Greta and Jeramie, may they get enough sleep before the baby, may they have an easy and fast labor, and may they get enough sleep after the baby."

They all downed their shots, as did Jeramie, put their glass on the table, finished their beer, and headed to the door. Wix headed to the bar to settle the tab. "What's the damage?"

"Well, it should be 154 Alliance credits, but I like you. So let's make it 130."

Wix pulled off some currency and put it on the bar, "Here's 150. So she gets the tip, better looking than you, mate."

Jeramie laughed. Wix dropped another hundred on the bar, "That, my friend, is for the baby. Start an account and let the little bugger have a nest egg to reach a goal in his or her life."

"Her life, Wix. And thanks." Greta said and kissed him on the cheek.

"We'll be back. I like this place. We're here for a week." He turned and left, joining the other two outside in the car. As he got in the car, he said, "I'm excited. I get to meet your Mom."

Winsin and Marcee looked at him like he was growing a third eye.

CHAPTER SIXTEEN

Marcee pressed the bell, and her mother opened the door a moment later.

"Marmar, I see you finally made it home."

"Yes, Mother, I had nothing else to do this week, so I borrowed an Alliance attack craft, grabbed my boss, and flew for half my leave to have dinner with the family."

From inside the house, "Finally. It has been months since your boss let you off so you could visit." Her father said.

"True, Dad, but he's not such a bad guy overall." Wix was laughing at the situation. They still had no clue he was there.

Her Dad continued, "Who's that with you, Mar?"

"Oh, him. He's my boss."

The looks on their faces were priceless. Marcee and Wix started laughing. Mom looked at her and noticed the ring on her finger. It took a moment to comprehend that her daughter was engaged, most likely with the man standing next to her. Then, her mother's eyes started getting damp.

"My baby." She hugged her daughter. Then, she looked at Wix. She had a spark of who he was and nearly jumped out of her skin. "Uh, are you my future son-in-law?"

"Yes, ma'am. I am." Wix said as Dad approached the door and saw the ring on her right hand. Actually, we plan to be married in Saruta if that's OK with you. My mother said not to worry about anything. She plans to bring in some planners or something to work with…." He smiled, "Marmar."

She slapped him on the arm.

Dad looked at Wix, "Are you, Wix?"

"Yes, sir. I am. I plan on marrying your daughter, too."

Mom had a revelation. "Is your Mother the Marzi?"

Wix and Marcee looked at each other; Marcee said, "She has something to do with leadership or something…." Wix took over.

"…Well, she does hang out with Marzo a lot." He looked up and rubbed his chin, "You know, I remember her telling me something about that."

"I've heard you call her Aunt Marzo," Marcee said.

Wix smiled, "You know. This is sounding more and more like…."

Marcee said, "Wait, she has to be. Don't we call her Mom-Zi?"

"Oh my god, you're right!" Wix said like it was a news flash.

Mom and Dad stood there with open mouths as the two went back and forth and started laughing.

After a second, Winsin appeared with their bags.

Dad said, "Hi, Winsin."

"Hi, Dad."

Wix looked at him sideways. Winsin said, "Oh, that. Not really. But our families were so close when we were young. Our parents were our parents. Collectively. There were five or six families, and we all were over each other's houses all the time. But Marcee's family, her house, this house; it was the central point of all our activities." He looked at Wix, "Brother Wix, welcome to the family. But PLEASE do me a favor and let me take you to visit my family. We joke with each other a lot, and a real joke like you popping into the house, well, I cannot pass that up."

"You got it, my friend."

"OK, gotta jet outta here. The life of a transportation professional is busy and constant."

Marcee gave him a hug, and Wix and Winsin gave a handclasp. Then, he turned and walked back to his car.

"Later, other parental units!" He said as he approached the car.

Under their breath, the parents said, "Bye, Winsin." It was barely loud enough to be heard, but Marcee and Wix heard it.

"Uh, Mom, Dad, can we come in, please?" Marcee said.

They all went into the house, and Wix looked around. Nothing like his childhood home since his Mom was a public figure and the second in command of the Alliance of Worlds.

“I love this place.” He said.

“So do I.” Marcee said, “Your Mom’s place is nice, but this is cozy.”

“Agreed. I need Mom to see this before the wedding. It is just the kind of home she always wanted.”

Her mother said, “You want to bring the Marzi to my house?”

“Well, where one goes….” Wix said.

Marcee said, “If the Marzi drops in, Mom, the Marzo will have to come with her. They do everything together.”

Mom looked at Dad, “How fast can we remodel?” She was joking, of course.

Dad fell in sync, “I will look into it tomorrow.”

They all started laughing.

~~~~~~~~~~~

Dinner started, and not everyone knew who Wix was. Finally, Dad stood and offered a toast.

“To my baby daughter and her future husband. This wine we are drinking was created by Winsin’s father. A hobby he and I share, but this one is my favorite.” He looked around the table, “Family. My daughter found a nice guy to fall in love with, and they have our blessing. I hear they plan to
~~~~~~~~~~~

marry here, on Saruta. That is fantastic. Let me introduce the couple, Marcee Morrow, my daughter, and her future mate, Wix Battle."

That did it. Now they all knew who he was, and a lot of gasps from the 14 people crammed around the table.

"WIX BATTLE!" Winsin said. "I thought that was you. You owe me cab fare!"

Wix, Marcee, and Winsin laughed hysterically, breaking the room's tension. Wix winked at Winsin and nodded slightly.

Winsin picked them up the day before and brought them to visit his parents. Nearly identical to meeting Marcee's parents. The three had a blast, and the parents joined in on the laughter since they realized Wix was not all high and mighty. He really was a regular guy. He loved being hidden in the background and letting others shine.

Her cousin asked, "I hear you got promoted to Major, dear?'

"I did, actually. The same day as Wix. Mom-Zi promoted us at a training session right after she was thrown on her ass trying to learn a new self-defense move."

Her cousin looked flabbergasted, "Mom-Zi?"

Wix said, "That is my fault. I make up names for Mom, and this one seems to have stuck. She likes it, but you can call her Droid when she comes to the wedding. Since her real name means toilet."

Marcee started laughing, "Granny B will never live that down. Naming her daughter toilet."

"Actually, Mom is cool with it. When she speaks, before the cameras roll, she mentions her name and how our cultures are so different but, at the same time, similar. Who on our homeworld, Earth, would have thought that the regal name, Andrea, would mean a toilet in another culture, on another planet, in another solar system, in another language."

Dad shook his head, "So what does she think of the humor around her name."

Marcee said, "She embraces it. But, she likes for close family and friends to call her by her real name."

"Great. I can do that, and I hope without laughing much." Dad said.

"Well, future Dad. If you do laugh, she will probably be laughing along with you," Wix replied.

The dinner went well, and the group of 14 killed off nearly a dozen bottles of wine. It really was good wine.

When dinner was over, they went into the living room and sat. Wix and Marcee sat beside each other, and a beep emanated from their pocket. They both looked at the message, and Wix nodded to Marcee.

She said, "Well, it appears that Mom-Zi has a state visit or something to Saruta tomorrow and is on her way here. So we told her to meet us at Greta and Jeramie's Pub for a drink, and you are invited." She looked at Wix, "You may want to let them know the Marzi is visiting their establishment for a beer tomorrow."

Wix sent a message to them, and they replied fast. He mentioned Mom would enjoy that scotch.

“Done. Winsin, you wanna pick them up at the spaceport and bring them to the Pub?

Winsin said, “Them?”

“Yes, Winsin, my Mom and Dad. Maybe my sister, too.”

“Sure thing. What should I call her?”

“Oh man, please,” Wix said to him, “When you meet her, in as serious of a tone as you can muster, ask her if she is Wix’s Mom. She will love it.”

Marcee nodded, “That will set her up to understand what the visit will be like.”

“Sounds like fun. I’ll be messing with the Marzi. I hope I still have a job after I drop her off.” He smiled at everyone.

They all stayed till late into the night and talked. They did take the quiet family gathering outside in the yard and started a small fire in the pit. They were becoming a family.

CHAPTER SEVENTEEN

Winsin arrived early at the spaceport, and as the ship was cleared to approach, he pulled up, exited, and opened the door.

Andrea walked to the car, “Are you our ride?” She asked.

Winsin got a look on his face, “Not sure, ma’am. I was told to make sure I pick up Wix’s Mom.”

“Wix’s Mom! Oh, dear lord. Wix and Marcee must think you are a friend if you say that to me. Where are they?”

“Waiting for you at the Pub. They like that place a lot. But he is nearly out of Wix’s favorite scotch.”

Droid whispered something to an aide, and he ran back into the ship and came out a couple minutes later with a bag. “OK, whoever you are. Take me to my baby.”

“The name is Winsin, ma’am, and I have known your future daughter-in-law since I was but a pup.”

“In that case, you can call me Droid.”

Everyone piled in and arrived at the pub a short time later. As she entered, Marcee said, “Mom-Zi!”

Behind Mom were Wix’s Dad and his sister.

Wix yelled, “MAX! I did not know you would be here.”

“Mom had a visit to Earth and picked me up. I hear you are getting married. I guess my invitation got lost in the universe or something.”

“We have not sent them out yet but set a date last night.” He looked around at everyone. “4 months from now. The exact middle date between our two birthdays.”Then he looked at his mother, “Granny B’s Birthday!”

Andrea started laughing. “When she figures that out, she’ll probably pay for your honeymoon!”

“Mother!” He needed her attention. “This is Jeramie and Greta, owners of this pub. We will have our pre-dinner here.”

“What’s on the menu?” Droid asked.

Marcee responded, “Food, I hope.” Greta looked shocked, but Marcee continued. “Greta and I were talking about that, and I think sampling local foods from our two worlds would be fun. In his case, it could be Earth and Rest Stop. Of course, we will need a good cargo shuttle to collect everything, and maybe a good chef from Rest Stop and Earth will assist in the prep.” She smiled at Droid, who knew what was coming next, “Mom-Zi, can I borrow your car?”

The room exploded with laughter.

After they all were seated, Greta put a shot of the scotch in front of everyone. Finally, Wix’s Dad stood, “Everyone. Please join me in a toast to the soon-to-be couple, my favorite son and his future wife, Wix and Marcee.”

They downed the scotch.

“DAMN!” He exclaimed, “This is good!”

They refilled the little glasses, and Marcee’s Dad stood. “My turn, I guess. My baby girl is getting married. Figures she would find not only an amazing kid but one whose parents live in the limelight.”

Wix’s Dad said, “Mom lives in the limelight; I exist in her shadow and love it!”

“Well then, in that case, I think that is the correct Earth reference.” They all nodded to him, “To their future together. May they never attain all their dreams, so they have something to strive for; may they never lose the feeling they love each other; may they visit occasionally and give us grandbabies!”

Droid yelled, “ To GRAND BABIES, here here!”

Marcee and Wix looked down at the table, put a hand on their forehead, and shook their heads. Greta walked over and put a hand on each of their shoulders. “I’ll keep you posted on the process.”

Marcee looked at Droid, “Greta is a couple months pregnant.”

She walked to Greta and handed her a card, “This is my private comm. Keep me posted. I like babies!”

Greta was floored. Wix said, “Mom, I guess that will make you the Aunt-Zi for the baby?”

Greta said, “I like that!”

Droid gave her a hug, “You need anything, call.”

“Thanks,” Greta said.

“OH, Almost forgot. When we heard you had a pub and I was on Earth, I decided to find something unique for you.” Her assistant handed her the sachel, “This is 150-year-old Cognac. I am told this is the best brandy in all of history.”

She handed Jeramie two bottles, then gave one to Greta, “After the baby comes, this is for you. I can’t say it helps much, but it doesn’t hurt.”

Greta accepted the bottle gratefully, then gave Droid the biggest of hugs. She whispered in her ear, “If someone told me I would be hugging the Marzi, I might have placed a wager against it.” They both started laughing.

Wedding planning commenced. For about an hour and a half, they talked about the wedding and the reception, well, mostly the reception. Then, Wix made a call to Aunt-Zo.

“Aunt-Zo, Marcee and I are getting married in 4 months, on Saruta. We would really like for you to officiate.”

“My boy, I would be honored.” She said.

Marcee added, “Thank you, Marzo. It will make my day even more special.” She had tears in her eyes. Droid walked up and gave her a hug.

Marzo said, “I see you have that woman there with you also. I assume she and your father will have some official capacity at this momentous event?”

“Yes, Aunt-Zo, after all, she will be the Mom-Zi of the groom. Wait until you meet my new in-laws, and we also have a few new friends here. A couple of them own a pub, another a transportation company."

"Then I guess I will not need to worry about my travel on the planet."

Winsin spoke up, "No, Ma'am. When you are here, I will be your personal chauffeur. Any Aunt of Wix and Marcee is….well, you get it."

She laughed. "Marcee, how is your project coming along." Trying to be covert about the real reason she is here.

"Splendidly, everything should be set in a couple of days, and we will return to the capital. When we return, I can fill you in."

"Perfect. Bring Wix and the Marzi, and we can all have lunch on my terrace. Everyone enjoys eating outside on that terrace overlooking the forest preserve."

"I shall. See you then."

Before Wix disconnected the signal, Droid said, "Marzo, can you put out a vague press release stating that my son is getting married? I have not had the chance to do it yet, but it will look better in your office than in mine."

"I will take care of it personally." She smiled, "Take care, have fun, and I look forward to meeting all of you at the wedding." She disconnected.

Marcee's Mom asked, "Wix, was that the Marzo?"

"Yep!"

"She will be coming here for the wedding?"

"Yep!" He paused a heartbeat, "She will be officiating, actually."

"Where will she....uh...will she..."

"Winsin will be her personal driver. She'll be staying at the hotel and most likely want to drop into the Pub for dinner the night before." He looked at Jeramie, "She likes to drink an Earth favorite. A spritzer."

"A what?" Jeramie asked.

"Good wine and a clear lemon-lime carbonated beverage. Refreshing, slightly alcohol-based, but pretty tasty, I hear."

Jeremy said, "Greta dear, order lemon-lime soda and some wine tomorrow."

"Yes, dear!"

~~~~~~~~~~

The next day, the next several days, Wix and Marcee spent their time at the facility. Marcee is learning the Maronz computer systems. Wix is brushing up on prototype weapons tech and providing hands-on combat training. His specialty and his favorite.

At the beginning of the session, he asked who their best fighter was. A woman was pointed out by several others, and he called her to the front of the class.

"What styles of fighting do you know?" Wix asked her.

"Mostly Sarutan, but a man here showed us some Earth techniques." She said.
~~~~~~~~~~

"OK, great. I have not been exposed to very many Sarutan styles. By the way, what is your name?"

"Protector Marcee." She replied.

"Huh. Same name as my wife-to-be. Let's see if you can fight like her." He got into a stance, "Attack!"

She did, and she threw Wix to the ground.

"That was amazing!" The rest of the group was shocked that she tossed him as she did. "Now teach it to me!"

She broke the movements into sections for the next hour until he mastered them. Unfortunately, once he did, she could not duplicate the throw.

He stood in front of her, "What is your full name?"

"Protector Marcee Languna."

"If I offered you a position on my team, would you be willing to join the Alliance Protectorate, gain rank, and move to the capital?"

She thought for a moment. No one else could hear what they were talking about, "Yes. I would."

Major Marcee walked in a moment later.

"Major, let me introduce you to Protector Marcee Languna." He smiled broadly, "She tossed me like an old rag."

Marcee looked at the Protector, "Languna. Southern region?"

"Yes, Ma'am."

“I bet you did!” She grinned and looked at Wix, “The Southern region has a style of fighting I have seen but not trained in. I hoped you offered her a transfer?”

“I did, and she agreed.”

“Wonderful. When you join us, your rank will be lieutenant, and you will be a self-defense instructor.”

Wix looked perplexed. Marcee, his Marcee, continued. “If she threw you, she is at least second roch.” Their new trainee shook her head.

“No major. I am the fourth roch.”

“Then you will be a captain when you arrive.”

They trained for a while longer, and Wix tossed his fiance like an old rag, then he taught her how. Then, he began teaching the group of ten Japanese karate, and they took to it like they had done it before.

The evenings were spent relaxing at the Pub or at one of the family homes. This has been the best working vacation he has ever been on, and sadly, they need to head back tomorrow.

Although relatively small, the attack craft has room for both occupants to lie down and sleep. Something they took advantage of on the long flight there and home.

Knowing that when they returned home, they had a week to train their counterparts, Granny B had the rest of the team up to speed on the bang and the boom, as she would call it; they planned and departed on schedule in that little ship, partially disabled, covertly entering an area of space that, if discovered, the only outcome was execution. They had a job, a mission to complete, and an Alliance to protect.

That was something they did not take lightly.

CHAPTER EIGHTEEN

The craft entered Maronz space without incident and approached the homeworld. Making it appear they were attacked, with pieces of hull missing, belching smoke, and no communications. If they scanned the interior, it appeared three injured Maronz life signs and a failing life support system is what they saw. Nevertheless, they were allowed to pass to the planet without challenge and headed for the spaceport. A slight diversion and they landed, in complete darkness, on the street outside their objective. Giving the appearance of an emergency landing on the road.

Teams A and B dispersed and planted explosives. Then, Team T entered the command center, did as much damage as possible, downloaded everything, and destroyed the interface.

Finally, after the teams completed, Wix entered the room and hung a sign on the door written in Alliance Standard. A simple phrase, "LEAVE US ALONE, AND YOU WILL SURVIVE." It was attached to the door with an antique dagger found on a dead Maronz officer after a battle. They hoped the dagger was well known in their society. Point made!

Reentering the shuttle, they launched. The total time on the surface was less than 4 minutes. The damage was extensive.

After launch, the entire area exploded. They planted small explosives everywhere on the street, in front of buildings, and in vehicles parked nearby; anyplace they would inflict maximum damage, but at the same time, they wanted to not kill a maximum number of people, and they succeeded.

They were careful not to kill nonmilitary combatants or civilians. But the building they destroyed with implosion grenades made it clear they had new weapons, technologies, and tactics. A spread of those grenades on the hull of a ship or in a torpedo would be devastating, and the Maronz knew it.

The Maronz left the Alliance alone, spreading out in the opposite direction, gaining strength and number, advancing their technology and knowledge.

An interstellar war is at hand. When; no one is certain. But it will happen when the Maronz feel they can defeat the Alliance. So until that time, the Alliance is keeping a watch on the Maronz. Before Beeker passed, he developed an electromagnet shielding that made the craft appear invisible, at least to scans. If you looked out a window, you would see it. Using this tech, they created a ship that orbited the Maronz moon. They planted a sleeper program in the gorilla attack that sends data bursts into space periodically and randomly. It was the collection of past traffic through the hub. The ship hidden on the moon received the data and processed it to see what they were up to. So far, nothing about the Alliance.

Still, the covert Alliance ship would maintain a constant vigil. They watched, listened, and waited. A crew of six, 90-day rotations, two every 30 days. It was a resupply mission and swapping out personnel. Over the years, the Maronz never noticed.

Marcee and Wix's wedding went as planned, and for the first time in the history of Saruta, one of their citizens married someone so crucial to the family. So naturally, the news media tried hard to get an interview with the couple, but they had a plan.

They would honeymoon on Earth and Earth's Moon. But instead, Wix sent a message to a reporter he met a few years ago. A guy who could be trusted to tell the truth and spin a good story.

He told him to be in a particular theme park in front of a very specific building on a certain date and time. Wix never received a reply, but the reporter showed up, just him and his wife. The four sat at a restaurant and completed a nearly 90-minute interview. His wife ran the camera, and he asked the questions. The interview made this reporter's career. He knew it. Wix knew it. Andrea knew it.

After the interview, he offered to put them up if they made it to the Alliance capital. Less than a year later, he said he was on his way. He and his wife spent nearly 2 months in the city. Hanging out around the Marzo, the Marzi, and the Battle families. They created a documentary about the Alliance leadership, which was seen everywhere.

Marzo realized this man was an honest reporter and offered him a position on her staff. A few months later, he accepted. In addition, they discovered his wife was an electronics expert and had a position as the technical advisor to Marzo and Marzi. Her job was to evaluate new technology and explain it to Marzo. At least, that was the description unofficially. So, officially, Marzo created the position of Lead Technical Advisor.

Wix was promoted a few years later to Colonel, and since they are a package deal, his wife is always promoted, at least the past two times, at the same time he is promoted. However, this time, his Mother did not promote him.

In the past couple of years, General Dryer took over as the head of Earth Military. Through the abilities of her military mind, she was taking over as the head of the Alliance Protection Service.

After arriving on the capital planet, her first order of business was to have a conversation with her favorite colonel, Droid, as she called her. Of course, knowing her position was way above her, they were old, close, and dear friends.

General Dryer walked into the bar Marcee and Wix frequented, and the place became so silent you could hear someone's stomach rumble.

"Where are they?" She yelled.

A woman near her asked, "Where are who, Ma'am?"

"I need Major Wix and Major Marcee front and center."

They walked up and saluted, reported, and stood there wondering what this was about.

"Attention to orders," Although it was a civilian bar, everyone knew exactly what that statement preceded. As a result, the room came to a collective, immediate position of attention.

“It is my distinct pleasure to promote Major’s Wix Battle and Marcee Morrow to the position of Colonel. You will both be offered a position commensurate with your new ranks.” She turned to the woman who responded to her initial question.

“Here, pin these on them.” So she did and felt proud to be a part of this.

Sarah looked at this woman, “Captain. What is your name?”

“Ma’am, I am Captain Mak Boch.”

“No, you’re not, actually. You are Major Mak Boch, my new adjutant. I need someone close who is not intimidated by rank or position. You responded to my question.” She turned to the two, “Colonels, please fix her rank.”

They took the major insignia from her that she had removed a moment earlier. Wix removed the Captain's insignia, and Marcee put the Major's insignia in its place.

“I have one more promotion, but I have no idea who to give it to; Wix, who in this room can replace you as lead for the special battalion?”

Wix thought momentarily, and he and Marcee whispered back and forth.

“You know I am waiting, right? And getting thirsty!”

“General, the Colonel, and I, conferred and decided my replacement in the battalion should be Captain Marcel Revel.”

"That is wonderful since that is also who these orders are cut for, BY YOUR MOTHER!" The room laughed. "Captain Revel, front and center."

The other Major insignia was used.

"Congratulations to you all, all four of you. How many here are under any of these four newly minted officers?" The room quieted, and all hands went up, and she continued, "It appears that the drinks, for the remainder of the night, are on the tabs of these four promotees." Then, the room erupted again, "Bartender. I really need the best double scotch you have available."

"On its way, General!" Came from the back of the room. "And I also hear that these four tip well, too!"

The general added, "THEY HAD BETTER!"

The rest of the night was a four-way promotion party. The Grannies and Droid walked in about 20 minutes later, "Did we miss it?"

"You did, but grab something; they're buying!" Sarah said to Droid.

"Perfect! Barkeep, what's the most expensive thing you have that my baby and daughter-in-law can pay for?

"Someone donated this really expensive cognac, and I hear it is the most expensive thing in the place."

"Excellent! Give me a double."

The four newly promoted officers were standing there, trying to figure out if they could scrape together enough to pay this tab, then when Mom-Zi ordered, they just sat at a table.

Droid and the general joined them at the table. The general spoke, “Well, kids, having fun at your promotion party?” No one said anything.

Droid said, “Never fear, guys. The general and I have your backs on this. Let them have fun because we have something for you four in a few days. You will each get to pick a second, so a team of 8. Let’s talk at lunch tomorrow, at my office. Bring your second.” She downed her drink. “This is really good.” She stood and waved a finger over her empty glass in a circular motion and around the table.

Marcee looked at the others and said, “Don’t tell them where we are having lunch. Let’s make it a surprise.”

“Surprise? More like a heart attack. I knew I liked you for a reason.” Droid replied.

A few minutes later, the bartender appeared with six double shots of cognac.

The general said, “To the newest colonels and the newest majors. May your life never get boring.”

Droid added, “To my kid and his awesome wife, my daughter now. You are definitely a part of this family, and I get to take advantage of two for the price of one.” Everyone seems to have laughed except for Marcee and Wix. They clinked and downed the glass.

All of them said, almost at the same time, that the cognac was great. The four started feeling better and entered the promotion party's spirit.

The party continued for a few more hours. Finally, they left a healthy tip after paying the tab considerably less than their imagination suggested.

~~~~~~~~~~~

“Colonel, why are we in the official office complex.”

“Lunch. I hear there is an intimate bistro here.” Marcee replied. She walked to a door and did not knock. They just walked into the office of the Marzi, Droid, you know, Andrea Battle. She, Sarah Dryer, the Grannies, the General, and Marzo sat at a huge table. They were all spaced out, sitting around the table with two seats at each compass point. Finally, the teams got the idea. They were a little slow this morning for some odd reason.

Wix and Marcee sat on either side of Droid, their seconds beside them. The others, the majors, sat next to Marzo with their seconds next to them.

Marzo spoke, “Before Beeker passed beyond, he created an EM shield. You cannot see it, but it is there. So we are protected, concealed, and can speak freely.”

Sarah Dryer took over, “The Maronz are testing their encroachment into Alliance space again, and they need to be spanked. We need to send them a warning. There are 4 attack craft, prototypes, on Saruta right now nearly completed.”

Granny B took over, “The weapons on these crafts are all new. I do mean completely new. For example, the implosion grenades used on their home planet will look like a kid's toy compared to a torpedo, but they will never see it
~~~~~~~~~~~

coming. The EM shield is covering it, making it invisible unless they have someone looking out a window."

Granny K started, "Your tactics are simple. Approach each ship you come across and plant mines on it. We think you can get in and out without being noticed if you get dead behind them and fly right up their ass. Then, they can all be detonated simultaneously at the press of a button. A crippling blow to an invasion fleet. I recommend the aft top just above and centered between the stream exhaust ports. Their ships are a lot slower than these four crafts."

Droids turn, "Timeline. Take a shuttle and head to Saruta. Three days after arrival, long enough for them to teach you the systems, head into orbit and out of the system after dark. You have accommodations locally, near the test facility, and within walking distance. Make your way to Earth for rations and a few days' leave. You will be at the secure area in Wyoming." She smiled, "Who here has not seen snow and a close to -40?" Three of them raised a hand, "Good, you will get a new life experience. Your standard clothing should keep you comfortable in that environment. Once completed, you are to proceed to Maronz Space. We estimate at least a two-month journey one way. Once you leave Earth space, activate the EM cloak."

Marzo spoke again, "We estimate this mission will have a duration of more than 6 months. So I am glad you are paired off in your groups, male and female, not for the dynamic but for the sanity. Males and females each have a unique ability to see things." She paused a moment, "Colonel Wix. Except for you and Marcee, are these groupings sufficient for a dynamic?" She smiled slightly, and everyone at the table joined her, "If so, I recommend you and Marcee trade seconds."

"Well, Auntie-Zo, you picked up on that perfectly. The second I picked and the second Marcee picked are mates. So, with our trading, four couples will travel on this mission. All of them, all eight of us, I would stake my life on their abilities."

The general said, "Consider yourself swapped. The duration of this mission, the close quarters, and the 'dynamic' possibilities all come into consideration on a mission like this. Those are not large ships. The only seclusion you will have is the restroom, and it is just a sliding tarp in a corner."

Granny K said, "You will have a set of comm frequencies available for intercom between the four ships. These frequencies are not in the standard set for any species. You will each also have a built-in ARC transceiver. A daily data burst to a specific channel on the ARC using an encryption and compression technique you will learn on Saruta in two weeks will allow you to send reports and messages that appear to originate from Terra. This ARC has an OFF switch on the transmitter. This makes it undetectable unless the data burst happens. In this case, the computer presses the on and off buttons for you, active in milliseconds. These are the first ships to hold portable ARC systems. You can download whatever entertainment you wish to your storage before you leave Earth. The receiver is always active, but the EM signature of the receiver is minimal. Unless someone is looking for it, they will not see it."

Granny B added, "By the way. If you are captured, you will each be issued a code. Enter that code into any keypad, and

15 minutes later, that ship will no longer exist, if you understand me." They all nodded. "The code is the same for all four ships."

This was unlike any mission ever.

Droid added, "One last thing. If you come across a Maronz craft in deep space, it does not matter what direction it is heading. Your orders are to destroy it. To them, one second, they will exist. The next, they will not. So it will be painless for them."

Granny B spoke philosophically: "A few centuries ago, a group of Munitions Specialists in the United States military, the U.S. Air Force, created a slogan if I remember my history. These men and women loaded planes with bombs and missiles for the destruction and decimation of the enemy. That slogan was – **"Allowing the enemy to die for their country."** She paused, "It fits here also. They want us all dead. Showing them mercy will only allow them to kill you first. So I expect you all to have lunch with me here on this patio when you return."

Marzo said, "May good fortune fall upon you."

CHAPTER NINETEEN

The covert team decided the transportation to Saruta would be by public shuttle. No one had ever taken it, so it was a new experience. Once on Saruta, they stayed at a lovely hotel with first-class accommodations. Marcee and Wix managed a little time with the family, and Winsin picked them all up on the last night and brought them to the pub.

It was nice seeing old friends. Greta had the baby a few months ago and called upstairs to take her to see her aunt and uncle. Greta commented that if you two are her aunt and uncle, what is your Mom?

Marcee snapped a picture and sent it to Andrea. A moment later, Andrea said she needed Greta's comm ID and address for the baby gift. Greta nearly cried but held it, and a few minutes later, Greta received a personal message from Marzi's private comm.

"Wix, your Mom just messaged me."

"What did she say?" Marcee asked before Wix could speak.

"She said she is sending a gift from the local baby store, and I can pick it up tomorrow. She wanted to know her name and signed it, Aunt-Zi."

Wix said, "Well, there you have it. Next time you see her, you can call her Aunt-Zi, as can your husband and daughter. When she starts talking, I guess."

Winsin added, "You did reply that her name is Amber, I hope."

"Oh, I do need to send that to her." She tapped the screen for a moment.

Winsin continued, "I only wish I could be there in school when they see the Marzi on the vid, and lil bit here yells out, That's my Aunt-Zi!"

The table laughed, and they all agreed!

~~~~~~~~~~

They departed just after lunch and headed toward Earth. Once out of the system, they increased to max velocity and were impressed with the available speed. Although, usually, it would be a nine-day trip on a ship this size, they should be there in a few days. In addition, they had food and water for the journey to Earth. Finally, Jeramie saw they had refreshments for their trip to Earth, unaware of the rest of their mission. They told him they were transporting a few attack craft into Earth Space for security reasons.

When they arrive on Earth, they will install a food system with more than a year of rations in various forms. In addition, there will be a water system that can extract hydrogen and oxygen from space, a planetary atmosphere, or possibly the tail of a comet.

While on Earth, they plan to tour a few places. After that, they hope to reach the Lunar surface and, if possible, Mars.
~~~~~~~~~~

But that would be a colossal waste of time. So, instead, the President wants to meet with them. After all, Wix is still the son of Andrea Battle, and Marcee is his wife. So the rest get to come along just because.

They are bound for a location in Wyoming where the area is secure. Once in Earth's orbit, they will wait near the moon for darkness to set on their destination and land. From here, they can see the gray line clearly. Once on the ground, they will secure transport at the base. The next day, lunch with the Earth President and training on the systems. A little sightseeing if the opportunity permits.

Everyone thought of bringing a few bottles of some adult beverage. Marcee knew the Earth President, Patrice McClanan, enjoyed Sarutan Summer Wine, so she picked up a case as a gift. She also brought a few bottles of her father’s and Winsin’s father's wine as a personal gift for the President. The others had a small collection of spirits they picked up on Saruta, the Capital, and managed to find what they were looking for on Earth. While they were on Saruta, they learned that the four ships could be connected, and they could all move between each ship. Again, it is designed as an emergency evacuation, but on this trip, it will help to maintain collective sanity.

The craft themselves were spacious, as far as a closet goes. The internal capsule where they live is predominantly cylindrical. If the floor was not flat, it would have a five-meter diameter with a length of 30 meters. Tip to tail, externally, the ship is 52 meters and has a thickness of 26 meters. Tiny wings protrude from the port and starboard. For atmospheric insertion, the wings will extend to 52 meters tip to tip, from the 26 meters in the space configuration, allowing it to land unpowered and absolutely silent if necessary. Effectively, an interstellar glider. The power signature is only slightly above background levels. With the EM shield, it is invisible on any known scanner for any race, including the Maronz.

The color of the ship is flat, space, black. Completely unreflective, and unless you look at it as it passes, you will never see it. If you manage to see it, all you will see is an empty space, a dark patch with no stars moving through your vision. The engines are self-contained and self-regenerating in the far aft. The ships are referred to as the Black Diamond class attack ships.

The little attack ships also have teeth. Each ship has in its arsenal 25 implosion torpedos and eight dual sets of particle beam emitters – port and starboard, fore and aft, top and bottom. 100 magnetic implosion mines they will be setting on the enemy ships as they see them. The mines are designed to arm as they attach and detonate instantly if they attempt to remove them. In addition, a unique low-level signal emanates periodically to send a position fix of the ship. Finally, suppose the ships congregate, move towards Alliance space, or appear somewhere they should not. In that case, they can be destroyed en masse.

As the mines are planted, the activation creates a sequential ID, and each of the pings from mines on their rotating and random transmission tells home where each ship is located. Mines begin with 100- or 200- or 300- or 400- which lets the command know which of the 4 crafts has attached the mine. Next, they are to rotate planting the mines. All 400 of them. Then, head home.

The requirement for the mission was to covertly have the ability to inflict mass damage on the Maronz ships if the need should arise, but at the same time allow the Maronz to be none the wiser to their impending doom.

The mines have an estimated life of 40 years in space, a lot longer than the expected life of the ship itself. Therefore, the Alliance is protected for the next four decades. The downside is that if several ships decide to attack and the signal is transmitted, there is no way to limit its effect. All ships, all mines, would detonate as the signal reached them. Best guess, if transmitted from the capital, it would take 9 days to get to the Maronz homeworld. In the worst case, the engine core and compartment would implode as the signal passes a ship. The end result would be, at minimum, a floating box with no power, communications, or life support. The maximum effect would be an engine core overload and instant and total ship destruction. If the ship is in dock or has landed, the result would be devastating.

The mission lasted 11 months, and the four sets all survived. There were a few close calls, and they tested the new weapons and provided a perfect test right out of the gate. As they left the SOL system, they came across a pair of Maronz battle cruisers heading towards Earth. They were still a month or more out but could inflict significant damage on the Earth system before they were removed from existence. Wix ordered two ships each to target the enemy craft. Each loaded two torpedoes. They flew 500 kilometers aft of their intended targets and fired simultaneously. Eight torpedoes all hit their mark. In a matter of seconds, that area of space was nothing more than micro debris.

They sent that report home that evening, and monitor craft was dispatched to watch Earth space. A station was planned in deep space, unmanned, and a massive sensor package to keep watch.

All 400 mines were planted, and each ship used between 17 and 22 torpedos. They learned the beam weapon cuts directly through the Maronz ship and that the improved hull of the Black Diamond class ship has minimal damage from Maronz weaponry.

In one firefight, the last one, ship three, was hit by debris and needed to join another ship for a few weeks while repairs were made in space. They managed to land on a small moon with a minimal atmosphere. Suits were not needed, but supplemental oxygen was. Unfortunately, the ambient temperature was 1°C, making it a bit chilly to perform the work.

Two ships stayed in orbit on opposite sides of the small sphere to keep watch. They managed to get the ship fixed, and on the way home, they could only maintain 2/3 of their max speed. The other three ships matched their speed and flew to Saruta together.

~~~~~~~~~~~

"Welcome home," Marzo said. She looked at the two whose ship was damaged. They had surgery, and their arms and hands were bandaged. "Are you all well?"
~~~~~~~~~~~

With his arm in a sling, the man replied, "Yes, ma'am. Although we were injured, we will all survive without issue."

His mate added, "It appears that Wix and Marcee are quite knowledgeable in the medical arts. The doctors told us the first aid we received made it possible for a full recovery."

"Very good," Marzo replied. "Perhaps we should add medical technology training to your regimen. It appears the more you know, the safer you are."

Marcee replied, "Marzo, I have already submitted that recommendation to command. I believe they are taking it under advisement."

Wix added, "It looks like my entire battalion will become a flock of nurses."

Marzo said, "All the better."

They had lunch. They all talked like they were friends.

At the very end, Granny B asked. "Anything to report?"

After an uncomfortable silence, Wix said, "The new toys are all in place. 400 places, to be exact. We returned because we ran out." He was not talking or conversing. He was reporting. His face was unemotional, and his eyes were cold. Andrea saw it in his eyes. It was a lack of humanity. Something in her son, in all of them, had been extinguished.

"Nice…." She responded.

Marcee added, "The pulse cannons are devastating. A single 2-second blast from one ship drilled through the hull and into their engine core. After that, there was nothing left. They were, quite literally, vaporized. It was instantaneous."

Marina Marque said, "We had a ship take evasive action as we approached, but the pulse cannons are fast to target. One shot took out their engines. We left them, but less than an hour later, there was a bright flash from where we had left them. We returned to that point, and the ship was gone. We found their black box, their log recorder. We removed it from space as we were certain they knew who did this to them. We did not want that information getting out."

Granny K asked, "How did they see you? Did the cloak malfunction?"

Marcus Revel spoke, "No. We think they just happen to be looking out the window. Saw us and started taking random shots since they could not get weapons to lock."

Droid asked, "Did any of their shots hit?"

Captain Revel said, "Yes. We were hit twice. A direct hit on the starboard wing and a glancing blow to the ship's underside. We sustained zero damage except for a small burn mark on the wing."

"Good." Droid said, "How many ships did you remove from their inventory?"

Wix spoke, "Before each engagement, we scanned the ship. A total of 64 ships were destroyed, containing 320 Maronz soldiers. There was one ship, a cargo vessel, that we also came across. It had three soldiers, and we refined the beam to a minimal size and experimented. We found with a minimum beam diameter and 63% power level, the beam created a 9-centimeter breach, and the occupants perished in less than one minute. No time to suit up or get to their life station. We boarded the craft, downloaded their database, and ravaged through their cargo hold after making repairs to the ship. They mostly carried water and some protein mixes, but nothing we could use. So we left it as it was and sat the occupants in their seats. Pilot and copilot, that is. The engineer was placed at the breech with the repair tool still in his hand. Essentially, they all died rather quickly due to the breach, and the engineer repaired the ship but sacrificed himself."

Droid stared at her son. "Wix." She felt for him, all of them. This was a traumatic mission. She hoped they could push past it. "Creative use of your tools at hand. You did well. Where did you program the ship to head to?"

Marcee answered, "We set the ship to head to the nearest Maronz outpost. They should have been there in a few weeks. The ship was programmed to stop and hold station two million kilometers from the outpost."

The silence was deafening. Loss of 323 lives. It was necessary. The Maronz are ruthless. They would never show mercy to anyone they consider a lower life form, which is everyone. If you do not destroy them quickly, you will die. So they, the team of eight, did what they had to do.

Grannie K had already scheduled them with the therapeutic discussion teams. Individual meetings for a time, then a group session for a time, and hopefully, they can all get past the facts of the mission.

"Who wants dessert?" Droid said, "I have cheesecake!"

Nuteq looked at Andrea. She felt what she felt in this. All eight of her babies were hurting, and she could do nothing for them.

~~~~~~~~~~~~

Marcus Samuel passed away one afternoon at his desk. His administrative assistant found him when she came in for her shift. When the call to medical happened, Rebba stopped Margaret at the door. She was disheartened that his daughter arrived at the office for the emergency. She was the Chief Medical Officer, but still.

As Margaret entered the room, she looked at her father. She had examined him in the past few years and knew he was growing a mild heart condition. She looked at him, and it appeared that he simply put his head back on his seat and fell asleep after lunch. There was nothing they could do except for a transplant that was not available. She knew it. Her Dad knew it. She did not expect him to die at his desk, but it was a fitting end to his extraordinary life.

Decades of service to the colony. Decades of service to the thousands of people living on Terra. He had a legacy. This planet. The people.

Tonya renamed Owl Plaza at Town Square a little. She renamed it to "OWL PLAZA at MARCUS SQUARE." The city council voted on it, and a unanimous vote passed it in less than a minute. Victor and the Handys remade the signs for the plaza and replaced them the next day. Gloria, Victor's wife, had a plaque made for Marcus' bench. He was sitting on that bench if he was not at home or in his office. Summer or winter, even in the rain. The plaque read,
~~~~~~~~~~~~

“This is the thinking and comfortable bench of Marcus Samuel. Please have a seat. Conversation has a way of finding answers.”

His loss saddened the colony, and some expected Tonya to take over. Not her thing. She told everyone over the video. Her recommendation was to keep it in the family. So, she nominated Marcus Jr for that position. He accepted, and the votes tallied to near unanimous as the votes poured in through the screens in everyone's residence. Of the 16,000 plus votes, there were six against. His brother and sister-in-law, sister and her husband, mother, and yes, Marcus Jr voted against himself. The remainder of the colony endorsed that they trusted him to lead the colony. His father had trained, educated, and shown him how to lead and show respect while simultaneously being the leader needed at that moment!

The funeral was massive. People from all over the Alliance came to give their final respects to a man who was there when Earth joined the Alliance nearly 70 years ago. Marzo Nuteq and the Marzi went to the funeral along with almost twenty-five thousand people whose lives Marcus touched. Then, finally, Marcus Jr took over a role he was destined for and trained for more than 2 decades. He was ready to lead, and the colony stood behind him in every way.

Marcus Jr, now just Marcus, led the eulogy. He spoke first.

“My dad, what a piece of work. He was nearly 110 years old, but you would never know it. He acted like he was still in his 80s. To his final days, can you believe he thought EVERYONE came before him? Can you believe that in his mind, EVERYONE was equal, everyone? That is just so, so, unique in the universe." He paused a moment and looked at his siblings. "Here's the kicker, the reality of his mind and attitude. That man instilled that in me so I could one day take his place. But, then, he dared to tell me that when I took over, I had to do the same for someone else."

They finally understood where he was going with these words.

"Marzo Nuteq, I want to personally thank you for my father since he cannot. He really loved you, like you were his sister. Since day one, the day he referred to as the invasion, he told me you two bonded over meatloaf. I have one question for you though, Marzo," He paused briefly, "Was it good meatloaf?"

Marzo Nuteq stood, "In the words of your father. Meh." And she twisted her hand back and forth a little like he used to do in a so-so manner.

The audience laughed; everyone had seen him do that, and they recognized it. Marcus continued.

"Dad and I talked about this day. He was, after all, an antique. His words, not mine." His brother and sister nodded and smiled. "Dad told me if I get all sappy and sentimental and start bawling up here when I talk, he will come down and pop me on the back of the head. Then he said he may just do that anyway." The crowd applauded. He started speaking again, "Dad was an amazing man. He was a great father........" He pretended he got popped on the back of his head, and many people in the crowd chuckled. His brother let out a giant laugh. No one except his wife knew what he would say or do in his talk. He practiced it several times at home, so he had it memorized and down pat.

He talked briefly about his father's favorite place in the Alliance and some of his favorite people, then stopped momentarily and focused on the Marzi. "My Dad loved the Marzi. He said he thought of her as a daughter. No really. " He looked at the Marzi and waved, "Hi, Sis!" He said. She waved back. "Dad said that she, if anyone else in the universe, can be trusted with your life. He told me to avoid getting on her bad side and that she will always be a friend." He pretended to be thinking to himself for a moment, "Oh, he told me NEVER to call her Andrea in public, so I won't." The crowd knew it did not bother her, so they all laughed. He had spoken to her on her flight here to ask if it was OK that he did this. He told her it would be a happy remembrance service, not a sad downer.

"In closing, I want to thank my Dad for being my Dad and teaching me how to be a friend, a leader, and…." He faked getting hit on the back of the head again, and the crowd laughed, "Damn, Dad, OK, OK. I really have nothing else to say, with one exception. The Marzi asked to say a few words, so please, Marzi …Droid. Sis, you have the floor. I suppose that would be Sis-Zi." Then, as if on queue, she stood and put her forehead into her hand.

Andrea walked up and gave him a huge hug. Then, he punched his upper arm. Then, hugged him again. He took his seat to her left and behind her.

"My friends, family, and those I don't know yet, well, it's just a matter of time. About a year ago, Marcus and I sat in Owl Square, where we are right now. We sat on that bench over there, which was built by his son Victor shortly after Nina landed and the town of Columbus was established. Why were we sitting there? Because that was a place, we both felt happy and content. It also may have been because we shared a bottle of some really expensive cognac." The crowd laughed slightly.

"He told me we would be here talking about him one day. He told me that if his son got sentimental, I was supposed to shoot him, but not too bad. I am so happy I did not have to do that, Marcus." She looked at him, and the attendees applauded. Then, when it quieted down again, "He told me something interesting. When he woke up each day, he was scared. Not because he led a planet, not because he had to make important decisions that would or could affect the lives and future of so many people, but because of the outcome of those decisions. He was always scared he would make the wrong decision and the colony, town, or an individual person may be let down somehow." She paused a moment, starting to mist up talking about him, and she looked at Marcus, and he winked. "He was…" She faked being hit on the back of the head, and the crowd roared. Mission accomplished. She looked at Marcus, "Damn. That does hurt!"

"My friends, Marcus said this was a time of joy. He may not have been there, but he understood the idea of a real New Orleans funeral. Music, drinks, food, and people talking about the 'Hey y'all, watch this' or the 'Hold my beer' moments. If you don't understand that, ask a human about it while we eat, drink, and talk about Governor Marcus Samuel the First when we break." She turned to Marcus, "Sorry, kid." He saluted her.

"Marcus has passed beyond, and he believed in the Almighty. God. A Deity. He said he tried to live his life in service to whoever God put in his path, and that day, I landed on Terra, and we walked around. He told me he could see into my spirit and that I was someone to be trusted." She grinned, "But when my group from Rest Stop started jumping onto the roof of the building and lifting cars, well, he may have guessed wrong."

"He was joking with me, of course, but in his honor, when I heard about his passing, I commissioned renaming the forested area outside of my office to be named the Marcus Samuel Memorial Forest. As have the leaders of all worlds, the Earth President brought a single species of tree or bush that can live together in harmony. That wooded area is quite large, thanks to all members of the Alliance. It will not be a place to look at from afar, but it will be used to teach children about the fun and excitement of camping and survival in your own hands. We call it Scouting on Earth, but I learned in the Alliance that a similar organization is called Youth Education and Leadership Training. It loses something in the translation, but you get the idea."

"There is one more person who wants to say a few words. Dayl Warrin."

She sat next to Marcus and kissed him on the cheek.

Dayl stood there a moment; he hated being the center of attention. "You know, there is one thing Marcus and I had in common, we dislike crowds and being the center of attention. Wow, double whammy!" He smiled, "Marcus called me into his office a LOT of years ago to let me know he was kicking me out of the colony but in a nice way. I remember looking at him like he knew something. He was right, of course. I wanted to leave and start a colony where the rules were more in line with how I thought they should be. He let me go, helped me, mentored me as a leader, and helped me start the new settlement. He even thought of a name for me, and no, it was not Warrintown like we named it in this universe. He came up with Alternateville. I remember looking at him and nearly falling off my chair, laughing. That is when I knew this was going to work out. We had his support."

"The members of our town brought a proposal to Michael and me a couple of days ago. He occasionally visited us, and we always ended up at the local pub, The Pub. I know it's not a very creative name, so the proposal was to rename it with something that meant a lot to Marcus. So the pub's new name in Warrintown is **The Alternateville Pub and Grill**." Everyone laughed, cheered, and applauded. "I only wish we had some neon to light it up properly." He looked around, "Thank you."

"Dayl," Victor said. "You will have that sign in a week." They winked at each other.

As he sat down, something unexpected happened. It got a little sunnier, brighter. Everyone looked at the sky; they saw the star flickering a little brighter. It lasted only a few seconds, but everyone saw it. Finally, Marcus stood and took center stage.

"I guess Dad liked the memorial." Everyone looked at him as if waiting for his following words. He leaned close to the mic, "It appears Dad winked at us." Every person had

Marcus wink at them when something good happened, and they were together. This is another case of it.

The rest of the day was filled with authentic New Orleans music imported from Earth, thanks to those from the home planet. Marcus liked foods from every world he visited, which was his primary reason for traveling. A selection of his favorite adult beverages like beer, wine, and spirits.

After dark, well after dark, Marcus Jr grabbed a bottle of cognac as the party was breaking up and found Andrea. "Can we talk for a few minutes?"

"Sure thing." She ushered him to the bench, their bench, and now the bench of the son and her, "What's on your mind?"

He opened the cognac and took a long drink from the bottle, "I needed to talk to you because you knew my Dad better than I did. As a friend, not a son, or in your case, a daughter."

Andrea accepted the bottle and took a long drink. "I did. What shall we talk about, brother?"

CHAPTER TWENTY

Marzi Andrea 'DROID' Battle has been the Marzi of the Alliance for almost 26 years in Earth time and has loved working for the population she adores. Marzo Nuteq called her and asked to chat at her office.

Droid walked in, no knocking or announcement. She just busted in.

"Howdy." She said as she entered the room, thinking they would be alone. But, instead, she was floored when she saw the ten others, world leaders, sitting around the table on the terrace. "Did I miss something?"

"No, my friend. You did not miss anything. We purposely kept you out of this discussion until now." She looked at the table momentarily and then directly into Andrea's eyes. "I am retiring in a month."

"What?" she looked shocked, "Why?"

"Well, in your terms, my species lives about 125 years. I am 114 years old and ready to rest. You are considerably younger than me and have many more years to give." She stood and walked to her, "This group was convened almost a year ago to nominate a new Marzo. They shortlisted, as you would call it, five names. 3 from Earth, one from Saruta, and one from Praxit. Your name is at the top of that list. If you accept the position, you may select one of the others for Marzi."

"Uh.....I uh....well," She was speechless.

"I believe this is the first time in our history that the Marzi is speechless. Someone, please annotate this for posterity."

Andrea laughed, "Nuteq. Do you truly feel I am the right person to take your place?"

"No, not only do I feel you are the right person, but your decades of service to the Alliance, its people, and its member worlds have determined your fate, which is to lead them for a time. You are the logical choice. Not because you are currently the Marzi but because each Marzo has a particular mindset. When you see it in someone, you will know. When it is your time to step aside, and the humans say, you can depart knowing the Alliance is in good hands. You're the voice and the personality of the Alliance. And I can safely say, ANDREA, you have one hell of a personality!" Marzo does not use words like this, making Droid laugh.

The head of the nomination committee stood and looked her dead in the eye. "Marzi Droid! Do you accept the nomination to become the next Marzo?"

Andrea looked at Nuteq and grabbed her hand. She hugged her and looked at the committee members, one at a time, eye to eye. "President Suni Batal, I know you well. You know me. Before I answer, I need to know one thing. Was I nominated because I am the Marzi, and it is expected?"

Suni replied, “You are the first Marzi in over 200 years to be nominated for Marzo. The criteria are very specific, and no one can see them unless they are a member of this committee or the Marzo.” She took a step toward Andrea, “My dear friend Andrea. No, you were chosen because you checked all the boxes.” She grinned at her. “Let me explain. To be nominated for Marzo, you need to have accomplished specific tasks, have the support of the membership, be a household name for good, and have no ego. There is more, but you get the idea. No one put your name on the list, and we have met in secret for nearly a year waiting for this day. Finally, it is here, and we need your response.”

“I accept the nomination for Marzo of the Alliance.” Simple words with an intense report.

~~~~~~~~~~

“My friends. For the past year, a nominating committee has secretly tried to find someone to replace me as Marzo. I am stepping down. The transfer of office will occur a few days from today in this hall.” She nodded to Suni.

Suni stood and took the podium, “Members of the Alliance, leaders, and friends. It is with great pleasure that something that has not occurred in two centuries has happened. The new Marzo is to be the current Marzi. Although we know her as Droid, her actual name is Andrea Battle. On Earth, that is a regal name, and for decades now, she enjoys letting others laugh at the meaning of her name in the language of the Alliance.” She paused as everyone laughed at the thought.
~~~~~~~~~~

“She has accepted the position of Marzo, but that leaves a hole in the position of Marzi. Therefore, under the advisement of the current and future Marzo, the same committee has nominated Machi Borlin from Saruta for the position of Marzi.”

Machi stood and joined Droid at the front of the room.

Suni continued, “There is one last official act remaining. Voting to accept these two as our new leadership.” She looked at the two nominees, “All present. Do you agree that Droid Battle should be our next Marzo?”

The voting was green for yes and red for no. The time seemed to have stopped, and a minute passed, and then a green light, the size of a bus, illuminated.

“So it is voted, and so it is accepted.” She paused more for drama, “As for the Marzi, do you accept the nomination of Machi Borlin.” Another lifetime passed.

The green light appeared once again.

“So it is voted, and so it is accepted. Andrea ‘DROID’ Battle and Machi Borlin, four days from today, you will take your place as the new leadership of the Alliance.” The room erupted.

After it quieted again, Suni said, “Droid, please clean up your office for the next tenant.” She just about started laughing.

~~~~~~~~~~~

“As Marzo, I step down for the next. My role has always been for the good of all. I have not changed that, nor can I.”
~~~~~~~~~~~

She paused momentarily, “Three decades ago, she thought to talk to me, an invader into her space. A craft bigger than any Earth ship in their history and more powerful. She did something both expected and unexpected. She asked if I was an invading force or a friend she had never met. I am very thankful she thought to find out before launching weapons because, in her, I have found a friend that I have never had in my days. She speaks plain, sometimes too plain. She thinks before she acts most of the time. She is a diplomat when she is not playing with the military, getting thrown on her ass by her special team, or her son and daughter. Her husband, son, and daughter, and their families are like her. Her son Wix and his wife Marcee, generals and leaders in the Alliance, are from Earth and Saruta. He found her; together, they have protected and preserved the way of life we enjoy in the Alliance. Malaxi has been instrumental in creating, modifying, and dispersing technology and information to all planets in the Alliance. Her creativity, intelligence, and willingness to show others and let them shine are common themes in this family. Droid's husband, Marcus Reyez, is also one of them…. He tries to maintain a low-key appearance and refers to himself as the ‘first lady,’ a term used a few centuries ago on Earth for the wife of the male leader of a country who performed superficial activities. However, what he does is not mediocre. He has taken it upon himself to ensure all worlds in the Alliance are fed, clothed, and safe. His primary charity is a fund to aid new entries into the Alliance to show them they are welcome and that we share everything freely and without expectation.”

She paused a moment to let the family review sink in. She continued, "Our new Marzi is no better. He also does all for the Alliance and the people, and for years, he worked under Generals Wix and Marcee. His first assignment was a covert infiltration of Maronz space to let them know we do not take incursion lightly. It will be dealt with swiftly and permanently. Lieutenant Machi Borlin learned about family, commitment, duty, honor, and service to the Alliance from the family members of the new Marzo. In a very odd way, the new Alliance leadership and family agree. Machi grew up on Saruta. He met his mate, his wife, in school. Living in the Southern region has distinct advantages. It is more rural than the north, and he told Marcee he wanted to live in the north to see what that was like. General Marcee, a Colonel, then assigned him to the northern capital of Saruta for one year as a recruiting officer after promoting him to Captain. He took that responsibility seriously and brought in many new members of the Protectorate. He took the task, the job, and the responsibility seriously. His mate and children, Rakkana and the twins, Meecha and Horan, are no less than dedicated to the growth and well-being of Saruta and the Alliance. Rakkana will randomly appear and cook a fine meal for the members of the Protectorate. Everyone knows her and adores her."

She looked around, "You see, my friends, the future of the Alliance is in good hands. Marzo Droid and Marzi Machi will lead you into the next period in the history of the Alliance. So one last time, I will say, the Alliance is in good hands."

A standing ovation and the windows could be visibly seen shaking by the thunderous applause of those in the room.

Once the crowd quieted and took their seats. Marzo Nuteq said, “Madame President, it is with sadness and joy I pass the mantle of leadership to my dearest friend Andrea Battle, more commonly known to the universe as Droid. But, as is a custom on Earth I have learned over my years, I STAND RELEIVED.”

She bowed to Droid, and Droid turned to her and bowed; they hugged, and Nuteq sat. Andrea took the podium.

“Nuteq, I spoke to the council this morning while you were preparing for this meeting. You are the first Marzo to retire in centuries. I wanted you to know how special you are and how much we all adore you. The council has created a new title and position for a retiring Marzo that I hope to earn one day. You, my dear friend, are given the title of Marzo Emeritus. On Earth, centuries ago, the distinction of emeritus was given to a soldier who served their term. It still roughly means this on Earth, and the title is still given to professors, leaders, and those who deserve the honor. You are Marzo Emeritus. The former holder of this office, having retired, must retain your title as an honor from the people you have served, from all members, past, present, and future. To my children, you will forever be Aunt-Zo. There are many children in the Alliance, and I have one here today to assist me in honoring you. Long, long ago, my son married. There was a beautiful woman and a man and a child. You were Aunt-Zo, and I was Aunt-Zi. Amber was and is the beautiful child of Jeramie and Greta. Jeramie has since passed beyond. She is also my assistant and has been for the past eight years. Of all the people I know, she can keep me on task and ensure I am where I am supposed to be. A true taskmaster.”

Nuteq said, “That, my friend, is no small task.” The room let out a collective chuckle.

Droid continued, “I sent Amber home to Saruta to find artists and philosophers to create a medallion deserving of the title Marzo Emeritus. Unfortunately, she was gone for weeks; I was so lost and had no idea what or where my schedule was, so I did what I enjoyed; I tormented my son and his training class.” She waved at Wix, “Hi, Wix.” He waved back, as did Marcee. “He’s standing over there with my favorite daughter-in-law.” Straightening her collar, “OK, back to business, I guess. Now, back to Amber. She was headed home, and it had been a while, so I told her to make sure it was good and done and bring it back. She had to wait for it, so I think she took a vacation but managed to accomplish it.”

The room exploded again, and Suni brought a beautiful and ornate necklace to the front and handed it to the new Marzo. She, in turn, gave it to Amber. Nuteq stood, and Amber put the medal around her neck.

“The chain is pure gold and titanium. I used gold because a century ago, the most precious metal on the planet Earth was gold. Its value was quite a bit in grams. On the other hand, we, the colonies of Earth, made everything out of titanium because we found a huge asteroid that landed, and roofs, pipes, and walls were fabricated from titanium. This, to me, represents Nuteq perfectly. Gold and titanium, gold because Nuteq is elegant, and titanium because she is the salt of the Alliance.”

She took a sip of water, “WIX! This was supposed to be water!” The room laughed. Wix yelled back, ‘Sorry Mom-Zi….I mean Mom-Zo.’ She continued,

“I would like to introduce my Marzi. He and I met a while ago while I was there for a wedding. We sat over a coffee in the ‘Little Café on the Corner.’ It's one of my favorite places, by the way. He told me his vision for the Alliance, the security of its members, increasing the number of worlds, and many other thoughts and ideas that I thought were insightful. Fast forward to a month ago, and I see his name on that list. I thought he would be perfect. Besides, he occasionally appreciates a little cognac to contemplate the universe.” Laughs from those in the room.

“As for me cleaning out my old office, well,” She glanced at Amber, “How does it look?”

Amber replied, “Well, we did as good as we could, but you have been there a long time and accumulated a lot of cra…. I mean momentos.” She smiled.

“Good save, kid.” The chuckles in the room meant they understood this was all staged. “Only one thing left to do. Serve lunch and mingle.”

The remainder of the day and into the evening, the new Marzo, the new Marzi, and the Marzo Emeritus stayed, talked, and mingled. The food was terrific. An offering from each member world in the Alliance. Something that represents them as a people. There were 71 tables set up with the name and flag of each world suspended above its food, drink, or dessert.

Andrea went immediately to the Earth table and looked over the desserts. She was looking for something specific. As she looked for Angel Food Cake, she saw many things that made her happy. She made herself up a plate of scallops, shrimp, and lobster, a large slice of Angel Food Cake, and a double scoop of really aromatic kimchi. Next, she walked past the Saruta table and saw Greta. They had not seen each other in almost a year since Jeramie's service.

Andrea put her plate on the table and hugged Greta. "Marzo, it is really nice to see you."

'Wow. So formal." She smiled back.

Wix walked up to them, "Hi, Roger!" Greta said, and they all three started laughing. Then, Greta said, "I see you got a new job. I hear it is better to pay, but the hours suck." Wix cracked up. Greta knew how to make Mom smile.

"I know, right?" Droid said, still laughing. "One thing for sure, though, when I talk, people listen now."

Wix shook his head, and Greta hid her chagrin, but she saw it. Nuteq was standing nearby talking to someone, "Nuteq, my son is making fun of me." Droid said loud enough for her to hear.

"My dear friend. How is this out of the ordinary?" She said, smiling, and returned to her conversation.

"Greta. I heard that you closed the bar."

"I did. There were too many memories there, and I would need to hire a new bartender, and I could not bear to see anyone else in his spot."

"I do understand. What are your plans?"

"My first step is to hit every world and taste what they offer. Jeramie always wanted to do that, so I can do it for him." She looked at her plate, "What is that?"

"That, my friend, is called Kimchi. It is from Earth, a country called Korea. Do you like spicy hot?"

"I do."

She handed her a fork, "Try this."

As she did, she said, "WOW! Hot but really good."

Droid told her, "When you find yourself and are ready to return to work again, come here and visit with me. I have a position I want to implement, and I think you are just the right person for it."

"Really?" Greta said.

"Really!" Droid replied. She picked up her plate as someone waved at her, "I need to run, but remember to come to me when you are ready."

"I will." They hugged again and headed in opposite directions; Wix stood there grazing at the Saruta table. His wife walked up and ate off his plate.

"You know you could make your own plate, right?"

"I know, but this is easier and more fun."

He winked at her, and they walked around, grazing a little on each table they passed. Quietly, to each other, they mooed and laughed.

EPILOGUE

A few months later, Greta walked into the Alliance HQ building and approached the security desk. The guard looked at her, "I'll tell the Marzo you are here."

"How do you know who I am?"

"Ma'am, I spent a lot of time and cash in your bar there, too, and watched your daughter grow up. I watched her while you went on errands."

"Malik, right."

"That's correct." He looked at his console, "The Marzo will see you now." He raised a hand, and a young woman stood next to Greta. "This, lieutenant, is a VIP. Please escort her to the Marzo's office."

The lieutenant led Greta to the office, knocked twice, and entered, "Marzo, you have a guest."

"Thank you, Lieutenant Gray. You are dismissed." She grabbed Greta and hugged her tightly, "Let's have lunch on the terrace and discuss how you can serve the Alliance."

"How I can what?" Greta asked, flabbergasted.

~~~~~~~~~~~
~~~~~~~~~~~

Nearly three years after Droid became the Marzo, Nuteq left this universe. She presided over the memorial and had a lousy time saying goodbye to such a dear friend.

The Alliance is up to more than 100 worlds now; some are colonies of current members, but still, they are their own world and govern themselves if they want to do so. Earth is beautiful again, and the Alliance watches each planet for natural and ecological issues like a super volcano preparing to blast the world into the Stone Age. They have averted several problems in the last few decades. First, the planets are more than willing to allow interference because the Alliance has no malice or ulterior motive in helping.

Wix and Marcee are ready to retire, but not quite yet. They and another couple volunteered for a long-term assignment at the Maronz watch facility. They will be the last set of watchers, as the Maronz are nearly extinct. A rival species did not take kindly to their encroachment and attack on their shipping lane and, therefore, attacked and destroyed every world and ship they came across. Marcee was reviewing the current log files transmitted. They are ordered to attack the Alliance, steal ships, and capture all they can. So she sent a squirt to the capital. They would be waiting for them.

The flagship's Captain, Colonel Martuu Darazi, called to the Maronz as they arrived at Alliance space. The Captain of the Maronz ship said surrender or die. He flipped a panel on his chair. “One last chance. Turn back to your homeworld, or I will destroy your fleet.”

“A small Alliance fleet thinks they are going to damage the Maronz. Let me see you try.”

“OK, I did warn you.” He turned to weapons, knowing the sound of his order would be transmitted through the communications system to the Maronz fleet, “Target as many ships as you can on the first pass.” He pressed the button, “FIRE!”

Most of the Maronz fleet exploded. It went from 800 ships to 100 ships in minutes. Some exploded, some were disabled, and others were disabled and had a hull breach. As ships exploded, collateral damage took out the vessels closest to them.

The Maronz Captain yelled, “WHAT HAVE YOU DONE?”

“Demonstrated new weapons technology. Protected the Alliance. Destroyed most of your fleet because of your arrogance. Essentially, my job.” He paused momentarily, “I like my job and do it well.” A slight pause, “Target the remainder of the ships and fire at my command only. You have one minute to leave here and head home, or the rest will be destroyed.”

Everyone on the Alliance ships knew he was bluffing. A select few knew about the mines, when they were attached, and by whom. But the Maronz had no clue. So, without another word, the rest of the attacking fleet turned around and headed home. War averted, or the war lasted less than 15 minutes, and the Alliance won.

Captain Darazi thought, “I wonder how it will look if the other ships with mines start exploding in drydock, land on a planet, or..." His thought trailed off.

“Open a secure comm to the fleet,” He said.

A moment later, “Open, sir.”

“This is Darazi. Situation closed. B and D wings remain and observe for a few hours. If they appear to be coming back to take some type of revenge, run. Everyone else, head for the barn.”

A few months after this event, a covert relay was designed and placed in the Maronz system. Wix, Marcee, and the other couple flew the surveillance ship home. They had been there 8 months.

~~~~~~~~~~

Malaxi took the position of chancellor of Beeker University on Earth. The college is located in the Johnson City, Tennessee area. Nestled in the mountains. She started there as an astrophysics professor, and the questions begin when her students realize who she is. She is polite enough, but that’s Mom; I am me, is her typical reply. As a chancellor, she can avoid much of that, but she still gets to teach a class or three when she wants. Being fluent in maybe 24 Alliance languages, her time can be stretched, but she really enjoys it. Her husband is the dean of the English department and speaks only a few languages. They have no children and are not in any hurry to have any. But as they travel in the Alliance, he is learning more.

~~~~~~~~~~

Terra and Rest Stop are doing quite well. They are a primary hub for transportation and a leading agricultural community of the Alliance. They have several colleges and universities on each surface, with agriculture and communications at the forefront. Romeo and Rebekka are retired now and live at the house full-time. They still help out when they can but enjoy traveling immensely. He and Rebekka showed up at the Alliance HQ one bright and cheerful morning and asked the guard if Marzo was free.

"I will check." The guard replied. "Her office would like to know who is asking."

"Please tell her she is the best downstairs maid in the universe."

The guard relayed the message, the odd message at that.

"Send them up," Was the only reply. So they were escorted to Marzo's office.

"ROMEO, REBEKKA!" The guard knew Marzo was safe and returned to the lobby. "Breakfast is on me." She said, and they all laughed.

They stayed a week at her home and toured the city. Romeo played with some fantastic comm gear, and Rebekka learned about medical advances. But they needed to head out; they had a reservation in Saruta, and neither had ever been there.

When they arrived, there was a car waiting for them. "Hello, I was personally told by the downstairs maid to be available for you during your stay. Now, where to first?"

"You know the Marzo?" Rebekka asked.

"I do, now…."

"We have no reservations anywhere. Where do you suggest?"

"I have just the place." So he took them to Marcee's family home. With her parents gone now, the place sits vacant, and he is the caretaker. "Do you know Wix and Marcee?"

"Yes, we do."

"This is her family home, where she grew up. It sits now, waiting for them to return on vacation, but it is empty. I will let them know you will be here for a few weeks. Then, together, we will have a splendid holiday. Who knows, maybe they can join us for a time."

~~~~~~~~~~

Warrintown grew and eventually merged with Columbus. Dayl passed beyond, and Michael took over and led them into the future. The fear, paranoia, and controversy are all dissipated. Leaving trust and friendship in their wake.

Many crises have been averted, and the Alliance moved ahead.

THE END
~~~~~~~~~~

About the Author

Chris Cancilla was born in Cleveland, Ohio, on the East Side, in an Italian neighborhood called Collinwood, near East 158th and St. Clair. He really liked growing up there and would not trade it for anything. The friendships he made in Elementary School at Holy Redeemer and in High School at St. Joseph (now called Villa Angela – St. Joseph's) are priceless, and some are still in force. For most of his youth, he worked in the family business, DiLillo Brothers Dry Cleaners, for his Grandfather Carmen DiLillo and at DiLillo Brothers Men's Wear for his uncle Tony (everyone called him the Czar). He also "apprenticed" with his Uncle Duke, an old-school radio and TV repair shop between the men's wear store and the dry cleaners. But he enjoyed working in the dry cleaners for his Grandfather the most. Two employees, Bertha and Evelyn, were like his second mothers.

In his youth, he really enjoyed Scouting. Spending a significant portion of it in multiple Cub Scout Packs, Boy Scout Troops, and Explorer Posts. Scouting□influenced his life positively, and the training, knowledge, and education he gained during his youth in the troop still influenced his decisions as an adult. The ideals of Scouting, especially the Oath and Law, serve him today as a moral compass, guiding his actions to be a man his family can be proud of in all aspects of his life.

After high school, Chris spent 14 years in the US Air Force, where he saw a large chunk of this 3rd stone from our star. One of his favorite assignments was to Lowry Air Force Base in Denver, Colorado, where he could ride motorcycles and camp in the Rocky Mountains. This is a close second to the 2 years he was assigned to and lived in Keflavik, Iceland. He and his wife Tammy became best friends and experienced odd and unique landscapes and adventures. One was the SCUBA Diving Club's Founding President at Naval Air Station Keflavik. The name of the club was:

"vörn kafara á Íslandi"

He and his wife Tammy live in Raleigh, North Carolina, close to Wake Forest. He really misses his little buddy and writing partner, his cat, Snip. Snip followed Chris around from room to room. You may or may not see him all the time, but he is always close by. Unfortunately, Snip crossed the rainbow bridge two years ago; he went fast, which was the only consolation. When Chris writes, though, he is still

close by. They made a paw print before he was cremated, and that paw print always sits on the desk near the computer.

The Boy Scouts of America is still a part of his life, especially in teaching new adults the skills needed to survive the outdoors and reinforcing how these outdoor skills and habits need to be introduced to the leaders of tomorrow. Leave No Trace camping is a significant part of his instruction and is a philosophy in the conservative style of camping Chris enjoys, if not the only way to ensure an excellent time for you and future campers. Wilderness camping is a great way to decompress and gain insight into what is hidden in the inner recesses of your mind. Sitting around a campfire on a cool or cold night, watching the flames dance, and watching the wood that has given its all to the moment's beauty allows you to reflect on your thoughts and be honest with yourself. The one person you cannot lie to is yourself, so honesty in your head provides nature to clarify all things.

Imagine you are asleep for a moment, and a noise wakes you. You realize you left the Dutch Oven on a picnic table, thinking you would clean it in the morning. Well, you spend the next few hours arguing with a 50-pound raccoon about the cobbler residue in the Dutch Oven on that picnic table, the same Dutch Oven you said you would clean up in the morning. Sometimes, you let the raccoon win!

Chris also has a passion for cooking. Creating several cookbooks allows him to experience new cuisines and cooking methods from around the globe. Still, it also gives him the ability and materials to share and teach cooking to less experienced or knowledgeable people. He does not consider himself a chef, but he does consider himself a somewhat OK cook, both in the home and in the woods.

Cooking in the woods is a skill that not all that many people have even considered. However, it is one skill that Chris enjoys teaching to Scout Leaders, both old and new, in classes he teaches for Scouters (Adult Boy Scout Leaders) and the Scouts themselves during the COOKING Merit Badge. Chris was happy that the BSA finally made cooking a required merit badge for the Eagle Scout rank. It is a skill that will be valuable for the rest of your life. Especially if you want to prepare a romantic meal for a date or simply provide a meal you enjoy.

Whenever Chris develops or finishes a new story or cookbook, he permits some people to read his book and offer ideas to improve the storyline or the text. In addition, he may allow you to be the next editor, for which he will give you kudos at the beginning of the book. Thus immortalizing you in the story for all eternity.

His last hobby is Amateur Radio. In the Raleigh, NC area, you can find him in the mornings on **K4ITL** and in the evenings on **AA4RV**; he pops in occasionally to AK4H. If you use a DMR (Digital Mobile Radio), try to make a QSO with him on the **TGIF Network, Talk Group 1870**. He usually monitors that talk group and would enjoy the QSO.

I hope you enjoyed reading this book. Please read others in the series or check out the cookbooks or both if you are interested in cooking. Also, pick up that briefing booklet if you work with an EDI team and do not understand Electronic Data Interchange. It is well worth your time to read. Reviews of those who previously read the book are in. It is a well-received and informative book that can help someone understand EDI's fantastic and fun world. Tell Chris what you think of the books you read and whether you liked the stories, the briefing, or the recipes.

Chris's day job is as an EDI B2B Integration Specialist or an EDI Developer. Take your pick; they both mean the same thing. He calls himself a digital mailman. He moves the data and information files from one place to another. Still, he does not own, nor is he responsible for, the data in any way other than delivering it. □ So, a mailman! That's a fancy way to tell someone you work with computers to translate data from one format to another. After all, the mailman doesn't write the letters but moves them from point A to B.

Additional Works by Christopher E. Cancilla

All these titles are available at: **https://AuthorCancilla.com**

The Archives, a 7-Part, Time Travel Novel Series

Revised, edited, and renewed as of October of 2023

1. The Archives: Part 1 – Education
2. The Archives: Part 2 – Fixing Time
3. The Archives: Part 3 – Salvation
4. The Archives: Part 4 – Family
5. The Archives: Part 5 – Fresh Start
6. The Archives: Part 6 – Continuum
7. The Archives: Part 7 – Temporal Logs

EDI Education Series, a 5-Part briefing **providing an understanding of EDI**

1. EDI Education: Briefing 1 – Introduction – What is EDI, and how does it work? Read and Learn!
2. EDI Education: Briefing 2 – Deep Dive – A Deeper Dive into the 850/Purchase Order
3. EDI Education: Briefing 3 – Getting Paid – a Deeper understanding of the 810/Invoice
4. EDI Education: Briefing 4 – Shipping – Demystifying the 856/Advance Ship Notice
5. EDI Education: Briefing 5 – The Complete Briefing – A review of the first 4 books with additional insight

Free to Read Stories

available on http://AuthorCancilla.com

1. Stargate Universe
2. Scorpion Sting
3. Terra Nova

Additional Science Fiction books available

1. The Ultimate Thru-Hike
2. Bus Route 40-A
3. Lost Earth
4. Colony 3

Books available in the Brigit Markz series

1. Mountain Life
2. Life in Transition
3. Home Life – *(Coming Soon, Spring of 2024)*

Other available books and novels

1. AMMO – IYAAYAS
2. Toasting Marshmallows on my Dumpster Fire
3. Getting Published
4. Getting Published Two
5. Life as an Amateur
6. Stories from Time and Space
7. Scouting and Camping: A New Parents Guide
8. Scouting to Summer Camp
9. Camp Menu Planning
10. Personal Menu Planning
11. Learning to Camp
12. Packing your Backpack for a 5-Day Trip

Discounts and Deals

For current and available discounts, go to http://AuthorCancilla.com

1. ARCHIVE: the 7-part series
2. EDI: The Complete Briefing
3. Learning to Camp and Learning to Backpack

Made in the USA
Columbia, SC
26 March 2024